Mirror Image

by

Lori Bell

This book is a work of fiction. Names, characters, places and incidents are the product of the author's imagination or are used fictitiously. Any resemblance to actual events, locales, or persons, living or dead, is coincidental.

Copyright © 2016 by Lori Bell

All rights reserved. This book or any portion thereof may not be reproduced or used in any manner whatsoever without the express written permission of the publisher except for the use of brief quotations in a book review.

Cover photograph by Lori Bell
Photographed on the cover, Abigail Stewart

http://www.brunswickme.org/departments/parks-recreation/parks-facilities/parks-natural-areas/
www.bluelight.org
http://www.timberlineknolls.com/drug-addiction/heroin/signs-effects/
http://www.narconon.org/drug-abuse/signs-symptoms-heroin-use.html
http://www.cnn.com/2014/02/04/health/how-heroin-kills/
http://news.nationalgeographic.com/news/2014/02/140204-philip-seymour-hoffman-actor-heroin-overdose/

Printed by CreateSpace

ISBN 978- 1532904899

DEDICATION

I believe people come into our lives at just the right moment, and for a purpose. Some, I've learned, are only meant to stay for a little while.

For all of you in my life who have remained a constant, for those of you who I'm just now getting to know, and for the one who gravitated back after we wandered apart.

Chapter 1

Isabelle Madden stood in front of the full-length mirror in her bedroom on the third floor of the townhouse on Freeport Street. Brunswick, Maine was where she had lived all of her life. It was the city known to be *beautifully balanced.* As Isabelle looked at her reflection, she should have seen a woman five-foot-eight with shoulder-length white-blonde hair, unblemished skin, and curves on a thirty-nine-year-old body which bore three children. *Beautifully balanced.* Instead, she tried not to stare at her mirror image of laugh lines and crow's feet or pay any mind to the additional twenty pounds she carried. She was striking, but she couldn't see it.

LORI BELL

At nineteen years old, Isabelle had gotten pregnant. She and Clint Madden had only been involved for a few months. His support was unwavering, and he promised to love her, and their baby, for the rest of forever. Now, twenty years later, that baby girl was in her second year of college.

Isabelle and Clint had undoubtedly struggled to stay afloat. Supporting themselves and their baby throughout their college years and the years that followed as they tried to settle into their respective careers wasn't easy, but they persevered. Today, Clint was the president of The Bank of Maine, and Isabelle was a guidance counselor at Brunswick Junior High School. Their daughter, Stephanie was unsure of what career path she wanted to pursue as she was nearing the end of her sophomore year at the University of Maine. Skylar, their fourteen-year-old daughter, already swore she would become a pediatrician because she adored babies. And then there was nine-year-old, Sammy. He either wanted to be a drummer or a stand-up comedian, whichever path fell into his lap the easiest would work for him.

Twenty years of marriage, three children, and two flourishing careers. Isabelle most certainly counted her blessings. Her life was not how she had ever imagined it, but she was barely nineteen when *her life* suddenly was no longer *her own* and any hopes or dreams solely for herself were gone. A baby had changed everything. Isabelle's children were her life. She laid in bed just a few nights ago and watched the movie, Mrs. Doubtfire for the first time in over a decade. She teared up when she heard actor Robin Williams describe to a divorce-court judge how his children were his everything. *I'm addicted to my children, sir. I love them with all of my heart, and the idea of*

MIRROR IMAGE

someone telling me I cannot be with them, I can't see them every day…it's like someone saying I can't have air. I can't live without air, and I can't live without them.

In front of the mirror, she was wearing white shorts that weren't too short, but ended mid-thigh to reveal enough leg. Her thighs weren't overly toned, but she had excellent genes which left her with a shapely body, natural muscle tone, and curves. She was wearing a powder blue peasant blouse with three-quarter length sleeves and a pair of white wedges on her feet. Her toenails and fingernails were painted pale pink. She spent a few more seconds in front of the mirror, contemplating on tying back her shoulder-length blonde locks, then opted not to. She left her bedroom and descended the windy staircase down to the main floor. She found Skylar lying on the couch, concentrating on her iPhone screen.

"I'll be back in about an hour, Sky," she stated, walking through the spacious open living room which was mostly all glass windows and French doors along the back wall. The room was naturally bright right now in the late afternoon hours of the day. Isabelle had enhanced that bright effect when she decorated the room in all white. A white sectional, two white recliner chairs, and a white shag area rug underneath all of the furniture. The flooring was dark hardwood and the tables near the furniture were all wrought iron with glass tops. "Tell dad and Sammy not to eat a heavy snack if they get here before I do. Dinner is in the slow cooker and we're eating early."

"What are we eating, and why early?" Skylar asked, sitting up to peek her head over top of the sofa to see her mother reach the front door and open it.

"Pulled pork on sesame buns," Isabelle responded. "Something quick because dad has a meeting at the bank and Sammy has a club soccer game." Skylar nodded her head of blonde hair, and resumed her position of lying down on the sofa. She, of Isabelle's two daughters, looked the most like her. Stephanie had her father's dark hair, high cheekbones, dark brown eyes, and olive skin coloring. Skylar was Isabelle's mini with blonde hair, blue eyes, and an ivory skin tone. Sammy was also a miniature replica of his father.

Isabelle made her way down Main Street, driving her Lexus GX 460 SUV. It was brand new and she thought it was too expensive and too flashy with its silver exterior and sepia leather interior. But, Clint insisted she have it. He enjoyed the finer things in life, and she did as well, but she didn't ask for them nor did she buy too extravagantly for herself. She remembered all too well the years they spent skimping and saving every penny earned just to be able to get by. She learned then how to reduce, recycle, and reuse efficiently. She still possessed those qualities even though they were now living beyond comfortable as a family of five.

Isabelle tugged at the ends of her white shorts as she stepped out of her vehicle and then slightly inched them back up as she was well aware of her lovies and attempted to conceal them inside the waistband. She thought of the weight she wished she could lose, but then inevitably shrugged it off again. She knew she didn't have the willpower or the determination to put the effort into it. At thirty-nine years old, she certainly didn't have a body like Gabi's.

Gabi Lange was Isabelle's same five-eight height. Her eyes were blue, her hair was just as long and equally as blonde.

MIRROR IMAGE

It was obvious she had aged better. Probably because she never married or bore children. She had all the time in the world for herself. Her body was toned and twenty pounds lighter as Isabelle now only dreamed of being. They were identical twins, born just one minute and a half apart, with Isabelle being first. The Lange women were striking. Gabi knew it, flaunted it. Isabelle never overly concerned herself with the mirror's image.

It was, however, so much like looking in the mirror when Isabelle sat down at the table in the little coffee shop on Main, where Gabi was already waiting for her. "This is the worst time to meet for a cup, sis," Isabelle told her, as she sat down quickly and plopped her handbag on the empty chair beside her. But, Gabi's text had seemed urgent just two hours ago, so Isabelle made it happen. For her twin sister.

"I promised to be quick," Gabi all but whined as she moved a plain vanilla latte across the tabletop to her sister. Isabelle knew that small, rich espresso would ruin her appetite for the early dinner she wanted her family to be ready for, but she started to sip it anyway. And enjoyed it.

"I'm assuming this isn't a crisis, considering you wanted to meet in public?" Isabelle asked her twin, looking around at how busy a coffee shop could be at three-thirty in the afternoon. There were people of all ages in there. It seemed to be a hotspot for teenagers after school. One particular couple also caught Isabelle's eye. She guessed they were retired, and enjoying life. She wondered, briefly, when she and Clint reached those years together, *would he share coffee with her on a late afternoon?* Life had become routine and certainly comfortable between them. Clint was a man she could count on. She never doubted that.

"Well, it's not the kind of emergency where I'm going to fall into your arms and burst into tears," Gabi replied, and Isabelle recalled the infinite amount of times she had. Over a man, typically. This time, it was her career. Gabi had found success in fashion design. She wasn't a millionaire with her very own personal dress line, which was simply stated, *Gabi*. But, she was successful. It was just going to take the right person, the right hands, for her work to fall into. Time and again Gabi wondered if leaving Maine was what it would take. The design firm in Portland, Maine, which hired her directly out of college, was where her roots were. Portland was only twenty-five miles from Brunswick, where her family lived. Gabi and Isabelle were as close as twins were said to be. Isabelle's family felt like her family. Being an aunt to her twin sister's three children was one of Gabi's greatest joys. "It is, however, life changing," Gabi added.

Isabelle tipped her cup to her lips and waited for her sister to continue. Gabi was a dramatic person, so hearing her out first was always a wise idea. "A major fashion house is interested in my line." Isabelle knew Gabi had offers before, but not one made her budge.

"Define interested," Isabelle told her.

"I will still hold the rights to the line, but I've been offered a half a million dollars to take it to the next level. That means I'll hand over my name and multiple designers will enter the scene and take a crack at it."

"Gabi," Isabelle spoke, trying not to come across as disappointed. "You said you would never…"

"Belle, hear me out please," Gabi responded, already

knowing this would seem as if she was selling out. "It will still be my name. It just won't be all of my work. The shell will remain, but the rest will be the imaginations and creativity of others."

"You're seriously considering this, aren't you?" Isabelle asked her.

"I would have signed on the dotted line already if it weren't for the location of the design firm," Gabi stated. "It's in Silver Spring, Maryland."

Isabelle set down the half-full coffee cup and pushed it away from her. She was done. News like this, if it were to in fact happen, would rock her world. "Gabi, that's something like ten hours from here. Please don't tell me you're moving…" The two of them had not been separated other than throughout their college years. They needed each other close by. It's who they were, or so Isabelle had always believed.

"It's nine hours and forty minutes," Gabi began. "Belle, I don't think I can pass on this offer. You know me. I've been sitting on my designs, my brand, for seventeen years. I make a very comfortable living, but I've yet to become a household name." Isabelle knew that's what her twin strived for. She wanted to be *somebody*. Her career was of utmost importance to her, so much so that she had never focused on getting married and having a family.

"Your mind is made up?" Isabelle asked her, trying to ignore the tears beginning to well up in her eyes.

"No, of course not. Not until we talk about this," Gabi said, feeling the tears surface in her own eyes.

"We *are* talking, and what I'm hearing is you've made a decision. You just want me to back you up." Isabelle had always been in her sister's corner, She was her greatest supporter, her biggest fan. But, right now, Isabelle could not bring herself to encourage Gabi to chase her dream. To leave. To move six hundred miles away. She felt incredibly selfish, but at the moment she didn't care.

"You know me, Belle. This isn't easy for me," Gabi spoke with her voice low and her eyes teary. Isabelle looked at her with compassion this time. Her beautiful sister. Gabi was the mirror's image for Isabelle, only perfect. "Why are you looking at me like that?"

"You are so perfect, and so is your life," Isabelle admitted, but it's not like she hadn't told her as much before. All of their lives Gabi was the one who had it together. She wasn't the one who got pregnant at nineteen. She earned her college degree four years after high school and immediately fell into a successful career. Isabelle, however, had to work for all she attained, while raising three babies. "You may look like me, but you're exterior is far more polished. Your career, your life-long dream, is on the verge of coming true and I'm sad for me. I don't want to watch you move so far way."

Gabi knew she had her sister's support now. This was more about them and their relationship. She felt the same way. She was torn about leaving. "Perfect is a word with entirely too much weight," Gabi began. "To me, perfection is feeling like the best version of yourself, and most of us continue to work on that. Perfection should never be compared to others. But, if you want to compare, I see you as the perfect one. You have a husband and three amazing children, a beautiful home with the white picket fence, and a career that fulfills you. Am I right?" Gabi asked, all but admitting she wished she had a family of her own.

"I am grateful," Isabelle replied.

"Of course you are," Gabi stated. "So, you see, we all look around and compare ourselves with who has what, who was blessed with incredible genes, who makes the most money. Perfect is inside us, all of us. We just have to mold it to fit us."

Isabelle smiled. "And you need to seize this chance to feel complete, don't you?"

"You know me best," Gabi nodded her head. There was no denying the sudden fire in her eyes, and Isabelle couldn't help it. She was happy for her, and wanted her to take the path now in front of her. Even if it meant their road together had forked. A little.

Isabelle stayed behind, alone in the coffee shop, after Gabi left for a meeting at the office. They hugged closer, longer, and tighter than usual, and when they parted Isabelle said she would leave soon. First, she needed to sit down again, alone at the table with her coffee that had gotten cold, and process this.

※※※

When she pulled onto the driveway, both of the double garage doors were open. She could see Clint's black Mercedes parked on the right side of the garage. Her door was open on the left and ready for her to pull inside. She didn't budge though. Isabelle kept her foot on the brake and left the engine of her SUV running as she sat stationary and looked up at the three-story townhouse with red siding. Red siding was obsolete on that street, and even in that city. That row of townhouses on Freeport Street, all detached from each other, certainly had a wide array of color choices for siding. There were powder blue, pale yellow, ghost white, and charcoal gray. The Maddens chose crimson red. Well, Clint had chosen red and Isabelle had just gone along with his preference.

This was their home. She and her husband had done well. Their baby who came along and changed their lives at nineteen was a young adult now, in college and embarking on a successful future. In just four more years, their middle child would be on the same path to higher education and attaining goals. Sammy had another nine years with them, and Isabelle suddenly felt grateful to still have a child. The idea of having an empty nest frightened her. Her entire adult life, all of their married years, had been about raising children. Even her job as a junior high guidance counselor circled around children. Isabelle suddenly thought of Gabi and she wondered what it truly would be like to just live in an adult world. *Would she be lonely?* She didn't even have a mere second in time to answer the question in her mind, nor did she want to, once the front door of the townhouse swung open and Skylar ran outside barefoot in short, frayed jean shorts and a snug florescent pink t-shirt. "Mom! You're home! Can we eat? Dad said the meat looks ready. Where were you?" The endless questions through her open car window on the driveway made Isabelle smile. She was home, where she was needed. For certain, she had taken the right path for her.

Chapter 2

Belle sat in her lawn chair at the in-town park, located on the banks of the Androscoggin River just below the Florida Power Hydroelectric Dam. Sammy was playing soccer there tonight, and what a beautiful evening it was as Belle appreciated the scenic view of the river in the distance. Fishermen were on the bank, and portaging around the dam with kayaks and canoes.

LORI BELL

A paved bicycle and pedestrian path along the river was active tonight as well. Belle thought about taking a walk on the two and a half mile trail while she waited for the soccer game to begin, but she opted not to when she heard someone mention that there were only ten minutes to go before game time.

Belle had changed out of her shorts and blouse, which she had worn to meet Gabi at the coffee shop. She was now wearing light, flared denim and a royal blue hoodie to match the team's color. She had taken off her white wedges and swapped them for a pair of dark brown Olukai flip flops. She could feel the grass tickling her toes now as the night air picked up and felt a tad chilly. She was thinking of Gabi, she had not stopped thinking about her since she broke the news. Gabi was leaving Brunswick, *and her*, Belle thought, and she felt pangs in the pit of her stomach again.

She hadn't mentioned anything about it to her family yet. Her kids were sure to be just as heartbroken. They loved their aunt. Gabi was a huge part of all of their lives. "Why so serious?" Belle looked up and saw Jacobi Elle planting her lawn chair beside her. Jacobi was petite at five-foot three, and her blonde hair was cropped short and spiked all over her head. Her makeup was flawless, her teeth were perfectly straight and bright white. Belle always enjoyed this woman. She was in her late fifties and retired two years ago as the Director of Guidance at Brunswick Junior High, where Belle worked under her direction for most of her career. She still saw her on a regular basis as her grandson and Sammy were club soccer teammates.

"Hey pretty lady," Belle said, as Jacobi leaned forward for a tight hug.

"Am I taking Clint's spot if I sit down right here?" Jacobi asked, before she made herself comfortable in the canvas red camping chair that she already pulled out of its drawstring-bag.

"No, he's wrapped up in financial meetings tonight," Belle stated. "You can be my soccer date." Jacobi smiled at her and sunk low in her chair. She too was wearing jeans, hers were skinny, and a team hoodie, with her feet in wedges like Belle had taken off. Jacobi always wore some sort of heel, not wanting to look *short*.

"Be my date afterward and we'll go to 7-West for a drink?" Jacobi had known better. She worked with Belle for fifteen years and never had been able to get her to tag along for a single happy hour. She didn't drink, she used to say, and no one ever questioned her.

"Believe it or not, I could," Belle admitted. "I had a disappointing afternoon." Belle thought of Gabi's plans to leave and there was no way around it, she was devastated.

"Oh dear, please tell me everyone is healthy," Jacobi practically begged, and Belle felt mildly ashamed as she realized she needed to keep things in perspective. No one was ill, and people and relationships did survive distance.

"We are all well," Belle began, "I'm just sulking because Gabi accepted a career move to Silver Spring, Maryland."

"Gabi?" Jacobi sounded surprised. "As in your joined-at-the-hip, already-made best friend from birth?"

"That's the one," Belle said, trying to force a smile. Jacobi was right. They were best friends. They shared the twin-bond, maybe even something stronger. They had friends outside of their close union, but it wasn't the same. Belle and Gabi knew each other inside-out. Their souls were one in the same.

"Oh, wow," Jacobi said, just as the game began in front of them. "You *are* going to need alcohol."

Belle sat on the sidelines watching Sammy succeed at his every attempt to keep the opposing team from scoring. As the goalie, he protected that target with everything he had. He dove. He jumped. He acted on every reflex and he stretched out his arms and legs as far as they would reach. He, for certain, inherited every competitive bone in his body from his father. Belle smiled, and felt the pride surface as she watched her son. And, then, from behind her, she felt two hands on both of her shoulders. She didn't have to turn around to know that touch.

Jacobi greeted Clint first, and he returned a friendly hello, standing there in his black dress pants and shiny black patent tie shoes. The sleeves on his white dress shirt were rolled up to the elbows and his red print tie was loosened around his neck. They talked about the score of the game, their team had earned two goals and the other zero. Clint mentioned his meetings were completed for the evening and Jacobi, partially joking with him, suggested how he should take his son home while his wife enjoyed a few drinks with her. Clint removed his hands from Belle's shoulders and she looked up at him to find that familiar expression. Clint didn't drink. He had grown up with an alcoholic and verbally abusive father, and he swore he would never touch a drop of that poison. And he hadn't for as long as Belle had known him.

She used to enjoy wine, but buying it and having it in their house always sparked an argument. Over the years, it just became not worth it to Belle to have a drink now and then. But, right now, the tension she felt over Gabi's decision to make a career move and leave Brunswick, made Belle yearn to escape her worry, her mounting fear of this actually happening.

A few hours later when Belle crawled into bed beside her husband, she wanted to tell him what was bothering her. He hadn't noticed she was quiet and feeling stressed. He wasn't the most observant, compassionate man. Belle made legitimate excuses for that. Tonight, he had meetings at the bank, and then they were wrapped up in their son's soccer game. Now that they were alone, however, Belle wanted to confide in him.

"I had coffee with Gabi this afternoon…" Before she could add more, Clint interrupted.

"Well that's a helluva lot better than drinking with Jacobi. Is she ever without alcohol in her system?" Clint was being his usual critical self on that topic.

"If you're implying that Jacobi isn't ever sober, you're wrong. She enjoys herself and who cares if that means she's a social drinker." Belle all but rolled her eyes. She loved and respected Jacobi and had always been unnerved at Clint's hurtful opinion of her.

"I'm just saying some things never change," Clint spoke, as he lied on his back, his wavy dark hair still wet from the shower. His practically hairless chest and slim torso were bare, as the white sheet on the bed covered his red boxer shorts to the waistline.

"Yeah, well, some things are about to change," Belle spoke with a defensive tone. She also was lying on her back, wearing only a white crewneck t-shirt, braless, and pink cotton panties.

"With what?" Clint asked, turning from his back to his side to look at her. Belle turned only her head and she had tears in her eyes.

"Gabi took a job in Silver Spring, Maryland. She can't pass it up. They want her line." The career move was going to be remarkable, but Belle still couldn't get past knowing her twin sister would be several hundred miles away.

"Damn, that's quite a change for her," Clint replied, surprised.

"And for me, for the kids, for all of us." Belle wanted to talk to her husband about this. How she was feeling needed to be addressed. This truly felt life-changing.

"It will work out, everything always does," Clint told her as he moved toward his wife, gave her a quick peck on the lips and then turned his back to her in their bed.

Belle reached over and switched off the lamp on the nightstand beside her. That was that. Everything always worked out because she went along with it. She never fought what life threw at her, she only accepted. Sometimes she had no choice, but mostly it was a learned behavior.

Belle was a good woman, a good mother, a good wife. No one expected anything less. Especially not her husband.

Chapter 3

Belle woke up to a text from Gabi. It was two minutes before six o'clock, one hundred and twenty seconds before the alarm would sound beside Clint and they both would wake up to start their day. She rolled over and brought her cell phone closer to her face. The phone was attached to the charger and plugged into the wall outlet so she had to stretch her torso the rest of the way in order to clearly read the text.

Call me before work.

MIRROR IMAGE

Belle started work at the junior high school at eight o'clock. She had to get up, shower, dress, wake the kids, get breakfast in everyone, and get out of the door together. Sammy had to be dropped off at the grade school and Skylar attended the junior high school where Belle worked as a counselor. Belle contemplated texting Gabi back instantly instead of calling before work. She wondered what was going on. Gabi never rolled out of bed before eight in the morning.

Is this about your decision to leave me? Belle smirked at the text before she sent it. Maybe she could guilt her into staying in Brunswick? She doubted so.

Yes. Run away with me.

Don't tempt me.

The two of them each giggled on their opposite ends.

Get ready and call me. I know how I will not have your undivided attention until you're wearing a bra. Gabi's text made Belle laugh out loud as Clint stirred awake.

Belle sent back an emoji smiley face with its tongue sticking out, and then she got out of bed and went into the shower.

As she was walking through the crowded school hallway, with white large-tiled flooring and dull gray lockers lining the walls on both sides, Belle was on her cell phone calling Gabi. "I feel like one of the students sneaking a quick phone call before the bell rings," Belle told her sister when she answered on the second ring.

"Oh you rebel you," Gabi mocked her good sister.

"What's on your mind? I have exactly twelve minutes," Belle stated as she turned into the guidance office, waved good morning to her secretary, and flipped on the light switch in her office as she entered and closed the door behind her.

"Have dinner with me tonight…" The first thing Belle thought of was Sammy had soccer practice, and Skylar had a science test that they had been studying for over the course of the past few days. But, these dinner dates would now become few and far between. Gabi was going to move and being available for each other on a whim, for dinner or anything, just would not occur anymore. Not as long as her twin sister, and best friend, was still going to move to Silver Spring, Maryland.

"I will make that work," Belle said, feeling sentimental.

"We have a lot to talk about before I leave," Gabi said, feeling melancholy as her career move was now official.

"We will always have a lot to talk about, Gab," Belle said, sounding like the older sister, factually by a minute and a half, for a change. "That's just us. It's our nature to never run out of words." Now, it just felt as if they were running out of time.

When Belle ended their call, she sat down behind her desk and sighed. Something just did not feel right. She was sad, and she could hear the uncertainty in her twin's voice as well. Once Gabi settled into her new career, things would get better.

MIRROR IMAGE

Once Belle adjusted to not having her twin near, everything would work out. It had to. That's the way life rolled.

Gabi sat on the burgundy leather sofa in her apartment, wearing her white fleece robe before she got herself ready for work. Today, after seventeen years, would be her last day working for the design firm in Portland, Maine. She felt hopeful for her line. This was her chance to shine. There was pressure though. A fear of failing she had never known before. She had to do this. She wanted to do this.

The businessman who hired her was in his mid forties. He was suave. He reminded Gabi of the Ken doll she was obsessed with in her Barbie doll collection growing up. Blond hair, chiseled facial features, and sun-kissed skin. He wanted her to be a designer on his team. She was beyond flattered. She was taken by him more than she had ever been with any man. She was charmed by his success. He was unbelievably attractive. Stunningly gorgeous. They had not known each other for more than a few weeks. And they were already lovers. She trusted him, and he counted on that when he introduced her to his way of life.

Wade Morgan walked out of Gabi's bedroom. His feet were bare on the light oak hardwood flooring. His silk black pajama bottoms hung low on his waistline. His blond hair was disheveled on his head, and the whites of his eyes were faintly bloodshot. He sat down on the sofa beside Gabi as she smiled at him and called him a *sexy sleepyhead*. He leaned forward, and placed his elbows on the coffee table in front of them.

It's how he started his day. Every day. There was still some of the white, powdery substance left in a small plastic bag.

He poured it carefully onto a tiny mirror in the shape of a square that fit into the palm of his hand. He used his finger to close one of his nostrils and he brought the substance underneath his nose and inhaled it all successfully with two attempts.

Wade already taught Gabi how snorting heroin gets the drug into the bloodstream immediately, within just a few minutes. The high from sniffing was also stronger, and does not wear off as quickly as using a needle. Wade was addicted to the rush, and he had been for almost a decade. He was a persuasive man. He had convinced Gabi to use. And she was already highly addicted.

Belle had a few issues at home before she was able to get out the door to meet Gabi for dinner. Sammy needed to be picked up from soccer practice and Clint was indecisive about being able to get away from the bank in time. Skylar was in tears because her science notes were confusing and the pages of information she had already memorized were lost to her again. Belle calmed her down, told her to get in the car and they would go over the information while they drove to the park to pick up Sammy at the soccer field. She told both of her children that there was dinner on the stovetop. They were to eat, do their homework, and take showers before she got home. Then, she promised Skylar she would quiz her over the science notes again later.

She was late for her dinner date with Gabi. When Belle finally backed out of the driveway, Clint was pulling in. She rolled down her window as did he. "Good! You're home. Eat with the kids and I'll be back as soon as I can." She tried to smile at him, but the look on his face, pure irritation, told her not to bother.

"I'm not sure why it's suddenly urgent to drop everything to have dinner with your sister," Clint said, obviously unnerved.

"She's moving, that's why," Belle felt sad just saying those words. She should not have to explain to her husband why she wanted to savor these last few days with her twin sister. She would soon be relocated too far away, and then the pain of missing her would settle in.

"I get that, I really do. Just don't be crazy late. We have kids who need you." Clint took his foot off the break and coasted up the driveway and into the garage. He never looked back. Clint Madden could sometimes be *a selfish ass.*

Gabi was waiting for Belle in a corner booth at Cameron's Lobster House when she arrived twenty minutes late. Belle had worn flared dark-washed denim with a peach tunic and dark brown ankle-wrap wedges. Gabi was still dressed in her work clothes, a lavender cami with a matching sweater shell, white linen crop pants, and strappy white sandals with a narrow one-inch heel.

"Sorry I'm late, apparently all goes haywire when mom has plans," Belle smiled at Gabi, and that's when she noticed a distance between them. The light in Gabi's eyes was missing. Their connection felt off. Her twin looked weary. Her eyes were what caught Belle's attention immediately. The pupils appeared constricted. Gabi's eye contact was fleeting as she looked at her menu and then lifted the glass of iced water to her lips. "You okay?" Belle asked her.

"Yeah, I am. Just a lot going on. Today was my last day at the Portland firm and…"

"Say no more. No wonder you look like you've been crying." Belle thought she had it figured out, but for the first time in their thirty-nine years together, she was way off.

When the waitress took their order, a bowl of Lobster stew for Belle, and grilled haddock for Gabi, Gabi added that she wanted a glass of Chardonnay. She rarely drank in front of Belle, because she knew her sister preferred not to, but tonight she felt like she needed more than iced water with lemon. "Make that two," Belle said, surprising herself and her sister.

The waitress gathered their menus and walked away before Belle spoke again. "It's a celebration, right? You are relocating and launching your brand in a whole new light. Great things lie ahead…" Belle was trying her best to be positive and encouraging.

"Right…" Gabi replied, desperately trying to conceal the fact that her brain and body were coming down from an earlier high. She had snorted heroin in her office today, to get through the emotions of saying goodbye. And, now, her mouth was dry and she needed a refill of her tall glass of iced water before she drank the wine she had just ordered. Her cheeks felt flushed as well.

Their wine came, their meal soon followed. Belle felt at ease after she began to drink her glass of wine. "It's been forever since I've had a drink," she told Gabi as she noticed her moving her fork around on her plate, but not eating much of her fish.

"You should cut loose more often," Gabi teased her, but meant those words. Her twin was too uptight. Too good.

"Yeah, unfortunately, my only friend in the world is leaving me..." Belle stated, feeling sad again. "So when is moving day, and how can I help? Clint will be ready to do what he can as well."

"You know I appreciate that, but it's already been taken care of. My new boss had a moving service in town today. There's nothing left in my apartment but a suitcase that I'll be living out of for two more days."

"You can't be serious. That's it? This weekend? That's some new boss..." Belle immediately felt as if there was more to the story than Gabi was saying. "Tell me about him. Is he attached?"

Gabi smiled, "Currently attached to me."

"That's what I was afraid of, Gab." Belle suddenly turned serious. "Why haven't you shared that with me? What happens if or when it doesn't work out between you two? Will your position in his company be secure?" Belle had so many questions as Gabi knew she would. That's why she had not told her. It saddened Gabi to keep things, important changes in her life, from her twin. But, now, she was in too deep and she actually believed moving, putting distance between her and Belle, would be best. She didn't want her sister to be disappointed in her. She was disappointed in herself. Trying heroin one time had been beyond dangerous. She needed help, she clearly realized that. But it was Wade she was listening to now. Not herself.

"I'm under contract," Gabi replied, confidently. She didn't add that Wade also promised to leave his wife for her. And she believed him.

By the end of the evening, Belle had assumed Gabi was physically and emotionally drained because this career change was taking an obvious toll on her. It had to be frightening as well as exciting. Belle could see Gabi had not eaten, and their conversation was all over the place at times. Gabi's concentration seemed lost.

They held each other close outside of the restaurant. "I will see you tomorrow," Belle told her. "You can stay with us the next couple of days, since your apartment is empty, if you'd like? The kids would love it…I would love it."

"I just might do that," Gabi told her, smiling sincerely. "I love you, Belle."

"I love you, too. Everything is going to be okay. Listen to me. Make this move, but if you hate it, if it's not for you, please come back. You can always come back home."

Chapter 4

Belle made it home in time to spend thirty minutes quizzing Skylar on her science notes. They sat on her bed and it was obvious to Belle that her daughter had spent the evening studying. She was proud of her, and told her so, as she tucked her into bed. Belle smiled at the long, loose blonde locks and blue eyes on a face that didn't look so much like a little girl anymore.

She then checked on Sammy, sound asleep in his dark bedroom. He had gone to bed without complaint, Skylar had reported, and Belle knew a busy soccer week had attributed to his worn-out state. Skylar had also mentioned that *dad was crabby*. Belle assumed she knew why. When she walked into their bedroom he was lying on their four-poster king-sized bed watching late-night television.

"Still awake?" she asked him as she closed their bedroom door and set her wedges down on the floor in front of her dresser.

"How was dinner? And Gabi? I'm sure she's all stressed out about the move." Clint was making fleeting eye contact between his wife and the TV mounted on the wall.

"I'm worried about my sister. She's not herself at all, but I can understand why." Belle sat down on the end of their bed, and Clint took his eyes off of the TV.

"Change is scary, but she'll make it. For a half of a million dollars, most people could handle it." Clint was clearly being snarky.

"I know she will," Belle said, ignoring his comment about the money, "but for the time being it's frightening to start fresh hundreds of miles from home. I'm sad, I know Gabi is sad, and well, it just sucks to lose her." Belle felt irritated with her husband's lack of compassion. He started to drift off to sleep while she was talking to him, so she ceased her words. She moved from the end of the bed and took off her clothes. She piled them up on the floor beside her shoes and slipped on a white t-shirt with her lime green cotton panties before she got into bed. Her own words were ringing in her ears as she laid down and pulled the sheet and duvet up to her chin. *It just sucks to lose her.*

Gabi was sitting on the bare hardwood floor in her apartment where her sofa once was. The room was dark. She had her designer handbag in front of her and the small plastic bag that was inside of it with the white powdery substance was now in her hands. She couldn't find her compact mirror, so she used a straw placed directly into the bag to snort the drug she had quickly and dangerously become entirely dependent on. She almost had not made it through dinner with Belle. She desperately needed a fix. She was so ashamed of what she had done to herself in such a short amount of time. She was a drug addict.

Within a few minutes, Gabi felt calmer and sleepier than usual. Without her mirror to visibly measure her intake, she had consumed too much heroin. She almost instantly had fallen asleep. Her body was hunched over the handbag on the floor. She was alone, Wade had traveled back to Silver Spring and said he would return for her on Sunday. Gabi's body's natural ability to breathe was abruptly thwarted. The heroin overdose caused her to succumb to immediate sleep, she began to forget how to breathe and her respiratory drive consequently shut down. In turn, seven and a half minutes later, her blood pressure dipped significantly, and her heart failed.

Belle had not been sleeping, she was just lying in bed with her eyes closed. She just kept thinking about Gabi and their life together. Her twin sister. Her best friend. In all ways, just as were her husband and children, Gabi was her world. The moment when Gabi Lange's heart weakly thumped its last beat, Belle's eyes unexpectedly popped wide open. She instantly felt alarmed. Panicked. Her own heartbeat quickened. Something was not right.

"Something's wrong!" Belle spoke aloud, and sat up suddenly, and then shot out of bed.

She rushed over in front of her dresser, pulling on the clothes she had taken off and dropped onto the floor earlier.

Clint sat upright in bed and asked her what she was doing.

"I have to go to Gabi!"

"What? Where? Now?" Clint was half asleep and confused. He thought maybe her phone had rang.

"She needs me! I can feel it!" Belle insisted, as she pulled on the last of her clothes and picked up both of her dark brown wedges by the straps and held them in one hand.

"Wait. Calm down. Are you sure you weren't just dreaming?" Clint wasn't convinced that it was necessary for Belle to leave the house in the dark of night to drive clear across the city to her sister. But, for the first time in a very long time, Belle wasn't hearing him. She wouldn't listen. She couldn't be deterred. She trusted this sense. It scared her too much not to.

"This feeling is too intense to ignore!" And those were the last words Belle uttered before she rushed over to the nightstand near her side of the bed and quickly detached her cell phone from its charger. She left the bedroom, running, as Clint laid back down in their bed, shaking his head. *What could possibly be wrong with his wife's twin sister at eleven o'clock at night? She had just been with her.* Clint blamed Belle's feelings on separation anxiety. And the separation was only just beginning.

✶✶✶

Belle drove frantically to the Riverside Estates. Before she reached Gabi's apartment building, she had tried calling her cell phone three times. The two of them had always been able to reach each other, even in the middle of the night. Belle was talking aloud to herself in her SUV. *What is going on, Gabi? Please, please be okay.* Belle had felt pangs of panic many times for her twin, throughout their childhood, teenage years, and especially their college years when they were separated. But, it was never like this. She felt an overwhelming sense of loneliness, and she didn't understand why.

She whipped her vehicle into an available parking spot, adjacent to Gabi's black 4-Runner jeep. She was home. At least she knew Gabi was inside of that apartment building. Belle threw her gear shift into park, her wedges instantly hit the concrete and she slammed the door closed and ran. There were two flights of white wrought iron staircases which led to Gabi's upper level apartment. Belle was out of breath once she reached the second one. She pounded on the door which had a Roman numeral nine on it. "Gabi, it's me! Open up!" Two more fist pounds in the dark, cool, outside air and Belle reached into her handbag for the key ring which held a duplicate of Gabi's house key. She fumbled with it, trying to see the key hole, and fit it successfully. Once she got it, she swung the door open wildly and it hit hard and bounced from the doorstop mounted on the trim at the base of the wall.

The first thing Belle did was flip on the light switch right by the door. And that's when she saw so much empty space. It was all floor and walls, and in the middle of all that space, on the floor, was Gabi. Partially sitting. Partially lying down. Slumped forward.

Belle dropped her key and her handbag at her feet, and lunged toward Gabi. "Oh my God, Oh my God, Oh my God!" Once she made it to her, she was on her knees beside her on the floor. Her eyes were closed. Her body felt warm. But, Belle could not find a pulse. "No, no, no! Gabi! Gabi! Stay with me!" Belle laid her twin sister down on the floor, flat on her back and began to attempt CPR. She screamed for help three times in between chest compressions and administering mouth-to-mouth resuscitation and finally a next door neighbor appeared in the open door way. He was a man who looked to be in his early fifties. He was shirtless and barefoot, wearing only a pair of gray gym shorts. She begged for him to *call 911, her sister was not breathing!*

Belle could hear the sirens in the distance. Her sister's neighbor was there with her, and they were taking turns, but finding no success with cardiopulmonary resuscitation.

There was no sign of life in her twin sister as Belle watched the paramedics take over. She kept talking to Gabi, begging her to live. In the midst of the emergent scene, a male paramedic asked Belle what had happened there. She suddenly became silent, showing signs of shock as she looked down at the floor where her sister laid lifeless. There was a white powdery substance all over the wood. There was a plastic baggie with more of that substance inside. And there was a drinking straw beside Gabi's handbag on the floor. It wasn't a mystery to any of them. Her neighbor was shocked. And Belle was confused beyond comprehension. *There was no possible way her twin sister, a person she shared her very soul with, would use drugs. There had to be more to this story. And, this story, would not end here. Belle would not accept it. Gabi would survive this. And there would be an explanation that wouldn't implicate her sister as a drug addict.*

Belle sat near and studied the scene. Gabi's strappy white sandals were off. Her white linen crop pants were wrinkled.

MIRROR IMAGE

Her lavender shell was almost all the way off of both of her shoulders and her matching cami was underneath the hands of the male paramedic, repeatedly applying chest compressions. She continued to stare at the paramedics as they relentlessly worked on her sister's body.

Chapter 5

Clint was there, beside her, but she didn't know who called him. *Had she?* He looked as stunned as Belle felt when the paramedics lifted Gabi's body onto a stretcher and then completely covered her with a sole white sterile sheet.

The police were all over the apartment, but mostly focused on the living room floor for the evidence. *Evidence of what? A crime? An apparent drug overdose?*

Her twin sister, her other half, was not a drug addict. That was why this, what happened in her apartment tonight, was unbelievable. Belle was numb. She never cried when the paramedics said *they were sorry, there was nothing more they could do*. Her twin sister was pronounced dead and Belle could not react, or feel anything. She should have thrown herself on Gabi's body while it still contained warmth. But she couldn't because she didn't feel a single emotion, except for maybe disbelief. That's was it. If she didn't believe it, it wouldn't be real.

Clint left her side and was talking to one of the police officers. She couldn't hear what they were saying, but she had tried to listen. Within a few minutes, the two of them were walking toward her. She was still sitting on the floor where she had been when the paramedics were working to save Gabi. Her legs were crisscrossed, her shoulders were slumped. Clint walked over to her and squatted down beside her.

"Honey, the chief, Michael Jones, would like to ask you a few questions." Clint's voice was gentle, and Belle couldn't remember the last time he had called her *honey*. She nodded her head, and she wanted to say she had no answers. She was looking for some as well. The Brunswick Chief of Police knelt down beside her and then he sat on the back of his legs.

"I know this is beyond difficult," he began, "but I really need you to focus on the last time you saw your sister. Your husband tells me that you had no idea she may have been taking drugs." The chief was careful not to accuse, cautious with his word choice. It was quite obvious to the paramedics and the investigators on the scene. There was an illegal substance on the floor, the woman was slumped over it and not breathing. But, to

Belle, and even to Clint, the scene was surreal. The reality of the end result was shocking. And, for Belle, it felt crippling.

"I had dinner with her just hours ago," Belle responded.

"And did she seem like herself?" Chief Jones asked.

"I'm sure my husband explained that she was preparing to move, she had taken a job offer in Silver Spring, Maryland," Gabi stated.

"Yes, that explains this empty apartment," he interjected.

"Gabi was tired, sad, and unable to concentrate at times during our dinner," Belle explained, thinking back that it couldn't have been entirely all about her move. But, how was she to know Gabi was feeling unwell due to drugs or needing a fix? It was the first time Belle had ever seen her *that way*, so she knew for certain she had not been using heroin for very long. Belle sat there thinking and the Chief was patient as he waited for her to continue. "My sister did not use drugs. I don't know what in the hell happened in the last few days or so, but her overdose was the work of an amateur." Clint nodded his head in agreement.

"We have your sister's cell phone," the Chief told her. "There are texts from you, possibly her girlfriends, and maybe even co-workers. There's one, a man by the name of Wade with no last name. Do you know a Wade?"

Belle shook her head no, and then she said, "Um, he could be her new boss…and they just recently became involved. Gabi told me so tonight. I had no idea, and we did share everything…"

"So your sister had been keeping things from you?" the Chief asked, and Belle hated, seriously hated, the way that sounded. But, it was true. Belle didn't know, until tonight, Gabi's new boss was her lover. Nor did she know Gabi had been using heroin. Belle knew the Chief was leaning toward this new boss, *Wade*, being the culprit. *Also a user. Or maybe even a dealer?* Belle felt a sudden rage, wanting to get her hands on *Wade* for what he had done to her sister.

"Apparently so, but that was not her. Not us. That's why this is so unbelievable to me." Belle shook her head and choked back a sob, and Clint rubbed her back with the palm of his hand.

"We are going to look into the fashion corporation first, possibly owned by this Wade, in Silver Spring, Maryland. We will trace the U-haul and retrieve your sister's things. We cannot bring back your sister, but hopefully we can put the person behind bars who led her to destruction." Belle never responded. She only stared as he spoke. "Just so you know, the story adds up. Your sister was new to this craziness, I believe that. Most heroin users live twenty or thirty years into using. The longer they do the drug, the less likely they are to die from it. They get it down to a science, so to speak." Belle didn't care. That kind of language was not in her world. *Drugs. Overdosing. Destruction. Accidental death.* She felt so pained, and when the Chief of Police finished his questioning with her, she remained seated, in that same place on the bare flooring, and physically could not move. She didn't want to transition to the next step. *Leaving Gabi's apartment for the last time. Going home to tell her children their aunt had died tonight.* It was all going to be too much.

When the officers were ready to leave, they told Clint he and his wife needed to leave the apartment as well. It was the scene of an official police investigation, so the door would be locked and police tape would be strung across it. There was *nothing left inside,* Clint told her, *and it was time to go home.*

"I can't," Belle managed to get those two words out. "I can't leave where she took her last breath. I knew. I felt it. I wasn't able to sleep, my own heart raced, I could only think of her, and I wanted to run to her. But, I was too late. I'll never get past this empty feeling…"

Clint was sitting on the floor with his own legs crisscrossed in front of his wife, still in the same position. "I know how it must feel right now," he began, carefully. "Let's just take the first step and get out of here. Together."

"I'll meet you at home," Belle stated, as a matter of fact.

"What?" Clint asked. "You are in no condition to drive…"

"I said, I will see you at home." Belle was adamant, and suddenly Clint gave in. What she didn't know was that he would leave the apartment complex and wait on the corner, near the end of the street. He would watch for her to leave, and then follow her home. *Did he trust that she could drive safely? No. But he was so scared of what would happen to his wife, now that she suffered such a tragedy, that he wanted to oblige.*

Duck underneath the police tape across the door as you leave, Belle was told by the final police detective to leave the scene.

MIRROR IMAGE

The room sounded hollow as the door closed behind the officer. The smell in there was different, too. It wasn't the usual perfumed Gabi scent, or the aroma of a vanilla candle burning. It was foreign and no longer a place where her sister lived, but now where she took her last breath. *Died.*

Just a few short hours ago, Belle believed she was being forced to say goodbye to her twin sister as she embarked on a new journey, several hundreds of miles from home. That seemed near impossible then to accept, to grasp. Now, the idea of getting in the car and driving to wherever her sister was didn't seem so awful. What was awful was this feeling that Gabi would always be out of reach. *Gone.*

Belle managed to get to her feet. Her legs felt shaky in her dark brown wedges as she stood. She walked over to the spot, the exact section on that floor where her twin sister lost her life. There was no emotion on her face. There were no tears in her eyes. She felt numb, but vengeful at the same time. *This man named Wade. He better hope the police are able to lock him away for the rest of forever. Because, if not, I will get to him.*

Chapter 6

Belle was seated on the end of the white sofa in the living room of her home. There was only one lamp on near her and the rest of the room was dark. Clint had gone upstairs to see if Skylar was awake. He woke her in a hurry late last night and told her there was an emergency with Gabi, and she would be there alone with Sammy until he and her mother returned home.

Belle watched her husband and two of her children descend the staircase in their pajamas, disheveled hair, and sleepy eyes. She took a deep breath as both Skylar and Sammy made their way over to her. Sammy sat down on her lap and Skylar snuggled close beside her. "Mom, what kind of emergency did Aunt Gabi have last night?" Skylar asked, fearing what she was seeing on her mother's face.

Belle had never been one to sugar coat the truth for her children. If something happened, she told them outright. She wanted to teach all three of her children, early on, that people make mistakes, bad things do happen, and never to judge anyone for their choices. Getting pregnant at nineteen had instilled that in her.

"When I had dinner with Gabi last night, she seemed sad and maybe as if she was feeling a little lost…" Belle began to explain to her children. "I assumed her plans to move upset her, I know she was scared to make a change that drastic. But, there was more. More, I did not know because your aunt did not tell me."

"She kept a secret from you?" Sammy asked, surprised.

"Yes…and that's something we never did. This time, Gabi was in trouble and afraid to tell me," Belle started to explain. This was incredibly difficult. She not only had to tell her children that their aunt had died, but *how* she died. That wasn't Gabi. She was a beautiful, successful, loving person who made a terrible choice, which cost her, her life. Belle still couldn't fathom it, so how was she to explain it? Clint stood back, near the staircase, and listened.

"She was scared of you?" Sammy asked, and Skylar blurted out, "No, Sammy!" She also had no idea what their mother was about to tell them, but she already knew it was bad.

"Sometimes we make choices and we worry about what other people will think," Belle explained.

"But you told us not to judge…" Sammy spoke, and Skylar interrupted again. "Sammy! Let mom talk. She has something very important to tell us!" Belle reached for her daughter's hand and held it.

"Gabi was taking drugs…the kind that are very bad for you, and she, on accident, took too many," Belle sighed as she spoke those words and prepared to say more, "and she died tonight." Skylar immediately began crying, and Sammy appeared confused. Belle felt in sync with Sammy. *Confused about why in the hell this was even happening.*

Belle held both of her children, and Clint walked over and sat down on the sofa beside all of them. This was the first time in several hours Belle had become emotional. Her children's pain had gotten to her.

Both Skylar and Sammy had questions, but Belle told them she did not have all the answers and she also admitted how she was just as stunned as them. When Sammy asked how his aunt died, *was there blood,* Belle's memory flashed to opening the apartment door in a rush and finding her sister slumped over and lifeless. "No, honey, there was no blood. She just stopped breathing and her heart stopped beating." Skylar cried again and this time Clint held her. Sammy remained seated on Belle's lap, still not showing much emotion, which mirrored exactly how Belle had reacted to this tragic loss.

✳✳✳

The funeral was a blur. Clint and Belle's twenty-year-old daughter, Steph, came home from college to attend, and Belle and Gabi's parents had flown in from Florida. Belle was heartbroken to see how losing their daughter had aged her parents overnight. They were in their early sixties and enjoying retirement, living in Florida.

Hundreds of friends and business associates had come to pay their respects to Gabi Lange. No one knew he was there, or who he was when he said he was a friend of Gabi's, and he never once gave his name. But, Wade Morgan was there. He managed to hide his shock when he came face to face with Belle, the identical twin. He had known about her. And then he saw for himself how she had Gabi's same face, tall frame, curvy body, only somewhat fuller. Wade was utterly heartbroken to see Gabi lifeless, to witness her family's pain and grief. He knew he was indirectly to blame. He also knew the police had no proof that he was the man who introduced Gabi to heroin. He covered his tracks well. He had for eight and a half years. He left the funeral home, and the City of Brunswick that day, with a sad heart. He truly had loved Gabi. She was different than all of the others. She was real. He wanted to give her the future she deserved and make her a household name with her fashion line. He never would have left his wife for her, he couldn't, but he did have hopes of sharing so much of his life with her, personally and professionally.

Wade Morgan drove his full-sized black Cadillac SUV through the gated subdivision to his mansion with twenty-something rooms, a tennis court, a pond, and a swimming pool. There was a time he could barely afford all he owned, and his lifestyle of needs and wants. And then he started dealing. Whatever anyone wanted, he sold. His undercover drug operation was intertwined within his fashion house. What could look like a business meeting on the third floor of his high rise was in fact a drug deal. Most of the interchanges, drugs for thousands of dollars, took place in broad daylight. That was Wade's niche. Blend and no one will suspect anything. He refused to deal from his home or on the street. When the sun went down, business hours were over. Tonight, he would be at home with his wife.

"Sonja?" Wade called out her name, but there was no answer on the main floor of his home. He called for the nurse, but he had not seen her car parked out front so he assumed she had already gone home for the day.

Wade made his way out to the back patio. His black slip-on dress shoes glided across the stamped concrete as the pant legs of his black dress pants blew in the wind. He walked over to the pergola on the far end of the patio that overlooked steps embedded in custom landscaping which wrapped around and led down to the swimming pool. It was the end of April and the weather in Silver Spring was unseasonably warm. The pool on the grounds still had its cover, and Wade made a mental note to hire to have it removed and the pool water treated. His wife enjoyed looking at, the pool relaxed her, she had told him numerous times. If the swimming pool water was heated, even on the hottest summer days, her physical therapist would be successful at getting her into the water. Those were good days, when Sonja was compliant.

Through the corner of her eye, she spotted him walking toward her. She was able to use her arms and her hands to turn the wheels on her chair to face him. From the waist down was the problem. Permanent paralysis ten years ago when she was thirty-five years old had changed Sonja Morgan's life. And the lives of her husband and son.

MIRROR IMAGE

After the accident, there had been irreversible damage to her spinal cord. The nerves within the spinal canal suffered blunt trauma on the vertebral column, affecting Sonja's spinal cords ability to send and receive messages from her brain to her body's systems that controlled sensory, motor and autonomic function. She didn't care about all of the medical nonsense. All she heard when she opened her eyes in that hospital bed following the accident was *paralyzed from the waist down, for the rest of her life.*

She had been walking on a sidewalk in downtown Silver Spring. She was in-between clients. Sonja was a licensed clinical social worker. She was committed to a career of helping others deal with issues involving their mental and emotional health. And what a cruel turn her own life had taken. There was no mind over matter left for her. Personally, she could not and would not help herself to overcome the adversity forced upon her suddenly and unexpectedly when a truck veered off the roadway and onto the sidewalk and hit her. She was trapped underneath a bench near the curb. Before she lost consciousness, Sonja remembered not being able to feel her legs. She woke up feeling the same way, and had ever since.

"Nice evening out here," Wade spoke, smiling at his wife.

"The weather. It's always a safe subject," Sonja replied, showing no emotion. Her long, dark, wavy hair was blowing back in the wind and her dark eyes looked sad. They always did. Wade chuckled at her comment, hoping she wouldn't notice how awkward he was feeling. He had just returned from driving nearly ten hours straight from Brunswick, Maine. His wife had not known he had been at a funeral visitation. She believed he was on just another business trip.

"I talked to TJ this afternoon, I called him. Caught him in the middle of studying for finals, but he said he could use the break. He's looking forward to spending a few weeks here at home before his summer internship begins back in Maine." Wade loved talking about their son with his wife. There was always a spark of something in her eyes when TJ was on the phone, or coming home to visit. TJ had his father's tall, toned build, but he was his mother's son. Dark brown hair. Dark brown eyes. And striking smile. When TJ smiled, Wade was reminded of happier times with Sonja. She didn't know how to smile anymore. She was in pain often, and no matter who tried what for her, she was drowning in self pity.

"It will be good to see him," Sonja replied, as she turned her wheelchair and began rolling it past her husband.

"Here, allow me," Wade said, attempting to take the handles behind her chair into his hands.

"I got it," she said, using the strength in her arm muscles to move the chair swiftly past him and onward, into their home.

Wade stood there, taking in the night air. It felt good to be standing, stretching his legs and back muscles after sitting and driving all day. He could not imagine being in his wife's place, although he had an awfully clear idea of it and would for certain trade places with her just to be able to see her walking, and living again.

Chapter 7

Steph Madden walked out of her biology class and into one of the campus courtyards. She saw her boyfriend waiting for her, and she smiled at him from a distance when he waved. His dark hair, dark eyes, and incredible build made her swoon. Steph thought she had been in love before, but those were just teenaged crushes. This, with TJ Morgan, was the real deal. She believed theirs was the kind of love you see in the movies, or read about in romance novels.

TJ was in his second year at the University of Maine also. He was already studying his passion in forestry and the environment. His father had found him the best school to focus on sustainable forests, the forest-based economy, and education in forests, wildlife, and the environment. The University of Maine was nationally and internationally recognized in its advanced wood composites, wood processing, bio-fuels, wood chemistry, and forest resources research. Learning in that location was ideal, TJ believed, as he was provided the unique opportunity of hands-on experience in Maine's own statewide forest and aquatic resources.

"Hello, beautiful," TJ said, kissing Steph as soon as she reached him. He didn't seem at all worried or affected by what the two of them were now faced with.

"How can you be so upbeat and carefree?" Steph asked him, with worry in her eyes. She had not stopped stressing and dwelling in the last few weeks since she found out that she was pregnant.

"It's all going to work out," he replied, taking her hand. "We just have to survive telling our parents…"

Just two days ago, Steph had been back home for her aunt's funeral. She decided when she heard the tragic, god-awful news that she would not add to her family's pain and stress right now. Compared to what had happened to her Aunt Gabi, it wasn't the end of the world that she was going to have a baby, but it felt like her life was ruined. This baby was life-changing, and she knew for certain her parents would be terribly disappointed.

MIRROR IMAGE

"I told you, probably a hundred times now, we will work this out," TJ said, but Steph wasn't entirely convinced, and she had yet to ask him to elaborate. What exactly did *working this out* mean? She was afraid to ask him if he wanted her to keep the life growing inside of her, the life they created. She wouldn't terminate this pregnancy. Her parents were pregnant with her when they were only nineteen and they made it work. She would not exist if they had chosen abortion. Steph would not be able to live with herself if she made a choice like that.

✳ ✳ ✳

Three weeks passed, and Steph was preparing to go home to Brunswick for the summer as TJ was only going back to his home to Silver Spring, Maryland for a few weeks. He had committed to doing a summer-long internship with forest resources research. They had agreed to separately tell their parents about the baby, given the fact that they lived six hundred miles apart. Again, TJ didn't seem as worried about revealing this news as Steph. *Of course he wasn't,* Steph thought, as she packed the last of her things to take down to her car in the campus apartments' parking lot. *He wasn't the one feeling sick to his stomach daily, almost all day long, and fearing how his body will change in just a matter of months.* She was not showing at all yet. Her tall, athletic frame would soon transform though, and the mere thought of it frightened her. She was a beautiful young woman. Dark hair, dark eyes, olive skin tone. She looked so much like her father, and TJ resembled his mother. Both were striking and made a perfect-looking couple. *A couple that would last through good times and bad?* Steph was counting on she and TJ's relationship to survive having a baby at young ages just as her parents had.

LORI BELL

✳✳✳

Four weeks to the day of Gabi's death, Belle felt as if she was walking around in a cloud. She had no clarity about anything. It took her forever to start and complete a single task. She had gone from an overachiever mother, who tried too hard to control her children's lives, to forgetful and slacking. She had completely lost interest in keeping her family afloat. Belle didn't recognize herself in the mirror anymore, and she truly had a difficult time staring at the reflection that once was a replica of her sister. She thought of Gabi day and night. Belle cried whenever she was alone and kept her feelings intact when her family was home. She hadn't returned to work and didn't plan to for the remaining two weeks of the school year.

Things had gone from bad to worse recently when the Chief of Police paid her a visit. No charges were being brought against Wade Morgan of Silver Spring, Maryland. The investigation into a possible drug ring came up empty. There was hearsay in that city about the fashion mogul, but nothing could be proven. All of Gabi's belongings, jam-packed into a single U-Haul trailer were returned to Belle. The police had gone through everything. Her death was ruled as an accidental overdose, and that was the end of it. A life well-lived for thirty-nine years by a woman who had so much more to give and be. But, most of the time, Belle felt as if she was the only one left to miss her. Her children were incredibly resilient to the loss and the change, and her husband was among the world that just kept going. Belle had yet to *get back into the swing of things*, as Clint daringly implied she needed to do, and for what it was worth, she had no desire to.

No one was at home as Belle made her way downstairs to the refrigerator they used for extras like soda, an additional gallon or two of milk, and the freezer was stocked with frozen pizzas and various ice cream treats. Belle squatted down in front of the open refrigerator door and reached far into the back for a wine bottle, which she had lying flat behind a row of Coke cans. She discovered drinking a glass or two of wine a day helped to calm her nerves. She missed Gabi fiercely. And she was terribly angry at her for being so careless and succumbing to such a dangerous drug. Belle wanted someone to pay. That someone was Wade Morgan.

She had done her research. Where he lived. She had taken down his address. She gathered that he lived with both a Sonja Morgan and a Thomas Jude Morgan. She assumed they were his wife and son. Belle spent hours reading articles online about Morgan Fashion, Inc. He was a successful business man, and in all of the pictures she had seen he was most definitely dapper and handsome, just as Gabi had expressed. The sight of him, however, sickened Belle to no end. He was responsible for the death of her sister. Indirectly, yes, but Belle didn't care about that measly detail.

Belle twisted the cork on the Chardonnay and retrieved a glass from the basement kitchenette. She sat down on the burgundy suede sofa they used to have upstairs in their living room before Clint wanted to replace it with something new. She tipped the glass to her lips and found solace in drinking alone in her basement.

She had lost track of time after she poured her third glass, and suddenly she heard someone descending the stairs. She felt panicked at first, and then thought, *to hell with it.*

"Mom? Are you down here?" It was her firstborn's voice. Belle had forgotten she was due home this afternoon. In what felt like another lifetime, she would have asked her daughter to call her when she left school and again when she was close to home. It was less than a two-hour drive but that was the kind of mother Belle was.

"On the sofa," Belle replied, and seconds later Steph came around the corner. Belle never stood up to hug her, and Steph immediately noticed her change in demeanor, and that she was drinking.

"Hi, um, are you okay?" Steph realized how silly, or maybe even insensitive, that sounded. Of course her mother was not okay. Far from it, and warranted, after losing her twin sister. Steph noticed her mother in jeans and a vintage white t-shirt. Her feet were bare with no toenail polish. Her shoulder-length blonde hair looked ratty from being uncombed or unwashed, and she was sans makeup. Her eyes were distant and sad, and seeing her this way deeply pained Steph. The mother, so put-together it used to annoy her, seemed lost to her now.

"I'm as okay as I can possibly be, considering..." Belle's words trailed off as Steph sat down close beside her, wearing a navy blue t-shirt with the University of Maine in bright pink lettering, and sweatpants in the same shade of pink. Her feet were also bare, but unlike her mother's right now, her toes were painted, again, in bright pink.

"I know you miss her," Steph began, "We all loved her so much. I still can't believe she's gone or how it happened. But, mom, you're drinking and sitting alone in the basement in the

MIRROR IMAGE

middle of the day. You can't do this to yourself." Steph sounded so grown up, and Belle knew she was right. She just didn't have the will to change her state of mind right now.

"I understand," she replied to her daughter. "I'm glad you're home, honey. I'll be okay. You just focus on college, your summer vacation, and your friends. You're young and should not pay any mind to your mother having an afternoon glass of wine. Don't tell your father, by the way," Belle added with a slight giggle and Steph wondered if she was tipsy. "So, tell me, anything new with you?"

Yes I'm pregnant, Steph imagined herself saying. She had mentioned meeting a guy at the start of the semester, but refrained from elaborating that she had fallen in love. Her parents had never met TJ, nor had they known she was seriously involved with anyone. They were certainly in for a shock, and Steph knew that was the last thing they needed right now. "I'm in love with a guy from school. His name is TJ. He's a forestry major. I've never felt like this about anyone, mom." Belle smiled sincerely at her daughter.

"That's wonderful news," Belle reached for her hand and took it gently into her own. "I'm so proud of you, the woman you've become. You are everything I wasn't at your age, confident and halfway through college without anything standing in your way."

"You had me in your life already when you were my age..." Steph said softly, with tears welling up in her eyes.

"And I loved you then more than anything...you must know that," Belle spoke. "I may not have been sure of a lot of things then, but that I always knew and I hoped you felt it as an innocent baby and now as a young adult." Steph was now in complete tears. She knew she had to tell her mother the truth and the only thing she was certain of at this moment was it would crush her.

"Please remember that I love you too when I tell you what I'm about to tell you," Steph repeatedly nervously. "Last month, I had to visit the urgent care center near the university and I called you for insurance information…"

"When you had strep?" Belle asked, and Steph nodded.

"It was irresponsible of me… I should have known that being on an antibiotic cancels out birth control," Steph said, waiting for the fallout. She could not even finish her words. And now she didn't have to.

"Oh my God!" Belle yelled out, and immediately put her hand over her mouth. "No, no, no. Please no. Do not tell me you're pregnant…"

Her tears alone answered that question for her mother. A steady stream down both sides of her face, which transitioned into a full-blown sob, left Belle feeling helpless beside her eldest daughter. The daughter she found out she was carrying at only nineteen years old. Steph was barely older than that and not ready for this life change either. But, ready or not, it was happening.

Belle set her empty wine glass on its side directly on her lap and she opened up her arms to her daughter and held her closely and tightly. She never cried, she just offered comfort to her little girl who was going to make her a grandmother before she turned forty years old.

MIRROR IMAGE

Steph was sure to remember this moment for the rest of her life. How it felt to have her mother embrace her when she needed her most. The unconditional love she received from her before a single word was spoken. But, most of all, Steph would carry in her heart how incredibly comforting and reassuring it felt when her mother whispered, "I am here for you and I will see you through this."

Chapter 8

Steph's question, *how are we going to tell dad,* caused Belle to fall silent. She sat there, thinking and coming to conclusions she didn't even want to imagine. Clint wasn't the most open-minded, worldly kind of man. He did, however, know exactly how it felt to be faced with uncertainties and diversity when he was nineteen and about to become a parent.

MIRROR IMAGE

The first thing Belle knew she needed to do was pull her household together. She hadn't done much around the house for several weeks. Laundry was always piling up, her kids and husband were washing their own clothes because nothing had been cleaned and returned to their closets and drawers. Their refrigerator was empty except for milk upstairs and her secret stash of wine downstairs. Belle told Steph to straighten up the house and maybe even run the vacuum while she went to the grocery store. They were making Clint's favorite meal for dinner tonight to maybe, hopefully, entice him into a good mood before he would feel like his world was turned upside down. Losing Gabi so shockingly and tragically had forced Belle into profound distress and sadness. Finding out that her daughter was pregnant had already, slowly, begun to give her a purpose. Or, at least, something else to focus on besides losing her sister, and herself.

She didn't have a list in her hand and that was unlike Belle, but she pushed her cart through the aisles at the grocery store and loaded a lot of everything into it. She was almost ready to checkout when she turned into an aisle, looked ahead and saw Jacobi attempting a smile, taking a few slow steps toward her. *What do you say to someone whom the whole town had been talking about and feeling sympathy for? When you're dear friends, as Jacobi and Belle were, you walk up to them and pull them tightly into your arms, without uttering a single word.* And that's exactly what Jacobi did. Being on the receiving end of that kind of embrace was so welcomed by Belle. She tightened her arms around her and paused a little while longer before finally pulling away.

"If only I could get one of those amazing hugs in every aisle of this grocery store…" Belle teased, smiling. And she noticed how good it felt to smile again, a real genuine smile.

"I would do that for you, you know that," Jacobi said, feeling worried about Belle as she had not responded to the multiple texts she had sent her.

"I know you would," Belle told her, "and you know that I appreciate how you have checked on me. I'm sorry, I just wasn't ready to respond or talk about it…"

"I understand," Jacobi said, "but you will be ready one day and that's when I want you to reach out. I mean that."

"This is the first time in weeks I've been able to get out like this," Belle admitted, and Jacobi noticed she had her hair up in a ponytail and was wearing no makeup. Her jeans and boxy white t-shirt with flip flops looked so unlike her.

"I can't imagine your house not being stocked with groceries!" Jacobi made fun of her Type A personality with a touch of Obsessive Compulsive Disorder, and Belle giggled.

"Well, imagine it. Steph is home from college for the summer, so I feel like I need to get it together a little." Belle didn't want to say more, but yet she wanted to confide in Jacobi. This unexpected news was something she would have called Gabi about already, as soon as she found out. And, now, Belle was feeling like Jacobi could easily become the next best thing. *A replacement? Never. But, a friend whom she felt a safe connection with.*

"How wonderful for you to have your whole family under the same roof again," Jacobi stated. "You need that so much now. But, I know how college kids are, she'll be out partying more than she will be hanging with the family at home." Jacobi chuckled, thinking about her fraternal twin sons who were juniors in college. Belle thought how that couldn't be farther from reality. She remembered all too well what pregnant at nineteen felt like.

"I have something I want to tell you," Belle lowered her voice, and Jacobi nodded her head and stepped in closer to her.

"Would you like to meet up later, after the kids are settled in for the night?" Jacobi didn't want to suggest *for a drink*, because this was Belle, but before she could add *for coffee*, Belle spoke.

"How about a drink? Maybe 7-West at nine o'clock?" Belle sounded so convincing that Jacobi never questioned her. Her eyes were wide in disbelief though as she responded, "Sounds good to me."

※※※

Spaghetti and meatballs with mixed greens were on the menu at the Maddens, and Clint was amazed by his wife's sudden turnaround. He did credit Steph's return and hoped this meant Belle would begin to put one foot in front of the other and be a wife and mother again. Picking up her slack in recent weeks had inconvenienced and annoyed him.

Both Skylar and Sammy were happy to have their sister home, and even happier to see their mom acting like she was feeling *better*. After dinner, Steph was the only one who remained in the kitchen to help clear the table and do the dishes.

"So, mom, are you going to tell dad? Or, are *we* going to tell him? I'll do whatever you think is best." Steph had not talked to TJ since they both left the university and drove their separate ways home. She knew he had a ten-hour drive, while she only had two, so she didn't plan to contact him until tomorrow.

"I think it's best if I tell him alone," Belle suggested, feeling certain, as she had thought about it all afternoon.

"Okay," Steph said. "Good luck."

"Yeah, I'll need some of that," Belle said, shaking her head.

"Mom, I'm sorry," Steph said. "I hate knowing I've disappointed you, and dad."

"I know the feeling, baby girl," Belle told her as they stood in front of the sink in the kitchen.

✳✳✳

All three of her children were on the main floor in the living room, watching a movie. Belle had already told Steph she was going upstairs to tell Clint the baby news. She also warned her she may have to keep her younger siblings calm if they heard Clint reacting in anger. Then, Belle added how she was going out later to meet a friend. Steph never questioned her mother, but she definitely recognized and felt caught off guard by the change in her. Belle Madden never went out. She ran a tight ship at home, and was the first to lock up the house, shower, and go to bed every night.

Belle walked into the bedroom she shared with her husband. He was sitting at his desk in the corner, his glasses were low on his nose and he was flipping through some paperwork he had brought home from the bank in his briefcase. He never looked up until she spoke.

"Busy?" Belle asked.

"Kind of," he responded, looking at her over top of his glasses. "I know what you're going to say...the kids are watching a movie and I should join them. I'd like to, but–"

"That's not why I'm up here," Belle interjected. "You need to take a minute and listen to me." Clint set the papers in front of him down on the desktop, and sat back in his chair. He never took his eyes off of his wife. She had changed in recent weeks, and while he was trying to be sympathetic and understanding, he just wanted the old Belle back.

"Our lives have changed drastically," she began. "I will never be the same." It was as if she was reading his mind, Clint thought, and he remained silent and attentive. "I don't want to be the same. I can't be, without my twin sister."

"I just need you to keep your head above water, for me, for our family," Clint stated.

"I'll need time," Belle said, feeling as if she was speaking to a stranger. The two of them had grown apart over the years. Or, maybe, they had never really been all that connected. Maybe they had gotten married because they had to. Clint loved her, she knew that, and he was committed to her. It was herself that she doubted. She had always done the right thing, what she was told to do. That now seemed tiresome to her.

"I know," Clint said, not knowing what else he should say. She did seem more put together tonight and he was relieved for that.

"I mentioned how our lives have changed, and I'm afraid normalcy, or what we were used to, is now a thing of the past. We are going to have to adjust and accept and open ourselves up to inhaling a deep breath and taking things one day at a time." Belle was babbling, trying to stall with breaking the news to him gently, if that were possible. "I want you to remember what we went through when we were nineteen, just babies ourselves, with a baby on the way." Clint looked puzzled.

"How could I forget that time? I was scared to fucking death," he admitted.

"You never told me that," Belle added.

"I was supposed to be strong, I wanted you to feel taken care of," he said, not taking his eyes off of her.

"You did take care of me, and our family," Belle said, sincerely, and suddenly she was reminded why she chose to marry this man. "And, now, twenty years later, I need you to be my partner in strength and support and love and guidance. We have to stay positive." Clint was a smart man and he could be perceptive when he wanted to be, but at this moment he was confused and uncertain by his wife's words. He did know she was preparing him for something.

"Steph is pregnant..." And that was not what he could have ever been prepared to hear. He removed his glasses slowly from the bridge of his nose and then he slammed them down on the desk. One lens for sure broke, but Belle took her eyes off of something that could be replaced and she focused on her husband.

"Son of a bitch!" he yelled. "Her life is ruined! She fucked up getting a college degree on time for sure!" Belle waited a few seconds longer, assuming there would be more to his reaction, his rant, his cursing. He was inclined to react however he felt he needed to, but afterward when the dust settled and the steam dissipated, Belle would need him to be calm, rational, and above all else, supportive.

"A college degree does not have a timeline. I was twenty-five when I earned mine, if you remember. Our daughter's life is not ruined. She's just going to have to alter her expectations now. You and I did so."

"Stop comparing us to her right now. It's far from the same thing!" Clint was angry, and Belle remained calm.

"No two situations are alike," she agreed. "But, what we do have here is our daughter who needs us. We've felt her same fear. We were on the receiving end of our parent's reactions. And, again, if you remember, that was hell."

"I thought it would be best to tell my father when he was already drinking," Clint recalled. "He hit me that night. He had always used abusive words, but never his fist. Son of a bitch."

"Exactly," Belle spoke. "Don't be like him. Be what Steph needs. Do not go to her downstairs tonight, or tomorrow morning, or next week, if you are going to lash out. That is not what she needs, and you damn well know that." Clint only stared at his wife. She had never spoken to him like this before, or told him what to do. She was in control and he wasn't sure if he was impressed or annoyed. "I'm going out tonight. A friend wants to meet to talk."

Clint had a look of sheer astonishment on his face. "You're what? Now? After what you just told me?"

"I told you I need the support of my husband and our daughter needs her father to be there for her," Belle said. "What you decide is entirely your call. Just know I will support our daughter no matter what." Belle started to walk away and reach for the door handle on their closed bedroom door.

"It's Jacobi, isn't it?" Clint called out to her. "You're meeting her to drink at a freakin' bar downtown…"

Belle turned back to him with a confidence he had never recognized before. "Yes, I am."

"You think I have not seen the wine bottles tucked inside the back of the fridge downstairs, or the empty ones in the recycle bin in the garage?" Clint asked her. "You know how I feel about drinking."

"Don't wait up," Belle said, before she turned her back to him, opened the door, and walked out without closing it behind her.

Chapter 9

It was ten o'clock at night when TJ made it home to the mansion in Silver Spring. He parked outside, stepped up to the archway of the massive front porch with four incredibly round pillars that not even a grown man could wrap his arms around. He knew, he had tried. When he opened the front door, most of the main level of the house was dimly lit. TJ assumed his mother was already in bed, so he walked up the stairs, hoping to find his father in his office.

He was wearing faded, relaxed-fit jeans, a red t-shirt, and navy blue running shoes. Those shoes squeaked on the wood flooring as he came to a stop in front of his father's open office door. Wade looked up from sitting behind his desk, and a smile quickly formed on his face. "Hey, boy! I was hoping you would make it in before I had to get some shut-eye." Wade rose to his bare feet. He was still wearing his black dress pants and his white long-sleeved shirt was completely unbuttoned and TJ could see his abs, which were impressive for a man of forty-five.

The two of them embraced, and TJ sat down on the end of the desk as Wade again leaned back in his black leather, cushioned chair. "Is mom asleep?" TJ asked.

"Yes, for a few hours already," Wade said, expressionless. "She'll be so happy to see you in the morning though."

"I know," TJ replied, wishing he could have back the mother he remembered up until he was eleven years old when the accident stole her ability to walk, as well as her spirit.

"So what's new? You're home for a couple weeks and headed back for the internship, forestry research, correct?" Wade was proud of his son. He initially expected for him to want to join the fashion business, but he never pushed him. He also, deep down, didn't want his son wrapped up in his other life. Drug dealing was not the future he wanted for TJ. Wade thought he had been discreet, protecting his son from the truth about his own addiction, but TJ knew. It was impossible to hide addiction when living under the same roof. And the rumors were always circulating about Wade dealing.

"Yes, sir," TJ replied. "There is something we need to talk about. Hear me out and help me, please." Wade nodded his head. He would do absolutely anything for his son, and TJ knew that. He also knew he could no longer go to his mother when he had a problem. And right now he had a crisis on his hands. "I met this beautiful girl at the beginning of the semester. She's amazing, dad. I love her." Wade smiled. He looked so much like his mother it was uncanny. Seeing the light in his son's eyes always made Wade miss the wife he used to know and deeply love. "And I got her pregnant."

"Whoa! Thomas Jude…you have got to be fucking kidding me!" Wade threw his arms back behind his head and dropped his chin to his chest.

"I wish I was, dad, but it's true and I don't know what to do…"

"I'll take care of it," Wade told him.

"I don't understand," TJ spoke, creasing his brow.

"Get your girl here, and I'll set her up with a doctor friend of mine. She'll only need a day or two of recovery. She can stay with us. I'll come up with some excuse to tell your mother." Wade was planning and plotting as if this was some sort of business deal.

"Wait, dad, no! You're talking get rid of it? Abort the baby?" TJ wondered if it could really be that easy. He also doubted Steph would see it that way. Or, maybe, she would if she knew he did. But, TJ wasn't even sure if he did. His father did. But, it wasn't his father's baby. It was his. TJ felt at a loss.

"It's the only way, son. You can't let your life come to a screeching halt because you knocked up your girlfriend." Wade was insistent.

"I'll talk to her," TJ said, feeling like his father could be right.

"Convince her," Wade added, "and I'll call the doctor in the morning to set up an appointment. Where does she live?"

"Back in Maine, only about an hour and forty-five minutes from campus." TJ never mentioned Brunswick.

"I can send a car for her, or buy an airline ticket. Just let me know," Wade said, and the subject was dropped between them like it really wasn't a big deal.

※※※

Belle ordered her second glass of Chardonnay before she told Jacobi she was going to become a grandmother. Jacobi took a long swallow of her Cosmopolitan before she spoke. "Oh dear Lord," she said, "You don't need this now."

"Neither does my daughter," Belle replied. "And, I know all too well what that feels like. My initial reaction was, *Holy Christ, I am going to blow a gasket*, and then it sunk hard and fast into my mind and my heart. I was there once too, at nineteen."

"You are an amazing woman, Isabelle Madden," Jacobi spoke, honestly. "I know what you've told me you went through and I'm sorry you will have to see your daughter struggle in some of the same ways. But, it's a different era now. Steph will make it. Does the baby have an involved daddy?"

"I don't know for sure," Belle said, feeling foolish. "Steph never told us she was dating. She loves him, I do know that. I'm sure we will be meeting him very soon. I want to see for myself what kind of young man he is, and if my daughter can count on him."

"That has to be strange, to not know much about him," Jacobi stated.

"It is a little," Belle agreed.

"How did Clint react?" Jacobi inquired.

"As well as can be expected, I guess. He was angry, but I was quick to remind him that he was there once too. I pretty much broke the news to him and left to meet you here. He seemed just as pissed that I was going out for a drink." Belle suddenly didn't care if she wasn't walking a line of being a good wife, or at least the wife Clint expected her to be. She was just now realizing that she had spent so much of her life, her marriage, pleasing everyone else.

Jacobi giggled and said, "I've been telling you for years that you need to let your hair down."

"I think I finally hear you," Belle responded, feeling different, and she didn't believe it was from the buzz she already had from drinking. Missing Gabi still felt surreal, day and night. She was suppressing her feelings, for sure. But, now, her focus had to be on Steph's pregnancy.

**

Steph woke up when her phone alerted her to a text. It was seven o'clock in the morning and TJ asked, *Are you awake?*

I am now, she sent back.

Sorry. We need to talk.

It's okay. Did you tell your parents?

My dad knows. TJ had confided in Steph all about his mother's accident and how she lost her will to live right along with the use of her legs. Steph knew he would turn to his dad first, but she hoped he would find the courage to tell his mother, too. She never saw her own father last night after her mother told him about the pregnancy. Steph was worried about today, when she would have to face him.

Was he mad?

No, supportive. He wants to help us, and that's what I want to talk to you about. Can I call you?

A few seconds later, Steph felt comforted hearing his voice. "I miss you," she told him.

"Then come see me," he suggested, and she giggled. "I mean that, come stay with me for a few days. My dad came up with the idea, actually." TJ was careful with his word choice, but he had to know how his girlfriend would feel about ending her pregnancy.

"Because he wants to meet me?" Steph asked, feeling loved and wanted.

"Yes, that, and he thinks we need to do the right thing for our future," TJ stated.

"I'm not sure I understand," Steph admitted.

"He knows a doctor here who can take care of you, um, while you're still not too far along…" TJ held his breath. If he knew her well at all, he knew she would not go along with what his father wanted, and had practically already arranged.

"What? You're talking about an abortion! TJ! We cannot kill our baby!" Steph felt sick to her stomach, which could have been morning sickness as well. This was something she would never, for any reason, go along with.

"Don't think of it as that," TJ began. "It could be the right choice for us, Steph. We aren't ready to be parents…"

"Twenty years ago, my parents weren't ready either, but they gave me life. How could I ever choose otherwise when I'm here because two people who loved each other chose to face anything because they wanted me." Steph felt teary as she spoke, but she was not backing down. This, if it came to it, would be her baby alone. TJ would have to make that choice. She imagined living without him as heartbreaking, but she would choose life for her baby over him if she had to. She was certain of that.

"I know, I know," TJ spoke nervously. "I will talk to my dad, again." As he said those words, he didn't know if he sincerely meant them, because he was now seeing this situation as his father was.

By the time Steph ended their call, she was crying. She hadn't agreed to visit TJ at his parents' home, not even when he persisted. He wanted her there, to meet them, but now she was hurt, scared, and disappointed just knowing TJ had been persuaded to abort their baby.

Belle knocked softly on Steph's bedroom door and then opened it. "You okay? I thought I heard voices?" She could see that Steph was crying and she didn't have to wonder why. She had been there.

"TJ called," Steph told her, as Belle sat down on the end of her bed. Belle was already dressed in a pair of mid-length white shorts and a long-sleeved button-down denim shirt. Steph was still wearing pale pink baby doll pajamas. "He told his father. They want me to come visit. His father knows a doctor who can help us. Mr. Morgan wants this baby aborted."

Belle stood up abruptly from the end of the bed. "You have got to be kidding me? Is this how TJ feels too?" Her mind was racing and the name Morgan rang in her ears for a moment. It was *familiar*.

"I think so," Steph started to cry again.

"Don't get yourself all worked up," Belle told her, reaching for her hand and Steph took it. "You are not making that choice. You know how I feel about that. End of story."

Steph nodded her head in agreement, and then Belle asked her something. "So TJ's last name is Morgan? I guess I didn't know what it was. Why don't you tell me a few more things I do not know about him. Where does he live?"

"Silver Spring, Maryland. His parents are married, but his mom is sickly. She was in an accident when TJ was eleven and it paralyzed her." Belle heard bits and pieces of what Steph was saying, but her mind pretty much halted on *Silver Spring, Maryland*.

"That's a far ways from here," Belle said, thinking of when Gabi told her she was making a career move there, ten hours from Brunswick. "That's a shame about his mother. What are his parent's names, did you say?"

"Sonja and Wade," Steph stated, oblivious to her mother's inquisition.

Wade Morgan. Wade Morgan. Wade Morgan. She had searched his name after Gabi's death. He lived in Silver Spring, Maryland. Two other names, she assumed were his wife and son, came up in her search as well as people associated with him. Sonja Morgan and Thomas Jude Morgan. *TJ, the father of her daughter's unborn baby, was the son of that bastard, the druggie, who took Gabi away from her. Forever.*

"Mom?" Now, Steph noticed Belle acting strangely. Her face had gone pale.

"Sorry, I'm just trying to piece together TJ's family. Eventually, I'm sure we will meet them." Belle tried to speak nonchalantly, but her heart was racing and the wheels in her mind were spinning. *Sooner, rather than later, she wanted to meet Wade Morgan.* She wished to see the shock on his face the moment he came to the realization that he will not get by with what he did, afterall.

Chapter 10

TJ had breakfast with his mother under the pergola on the patio overlooking the covered swimming pool two stories up. Sonja had a pale pink heavy sweater draped over her shoulders as the morning air felt chilly to her. Her frame looked even more frail to TJ than he remembered since he last saw her at Christmastime.

He watched her sip a hot cup of coffee and then pick at eating a piece of buttered toast. He had prepared himself bacon, scrambled eggs, and toast. He learned how to fend for himself a decade ago when his mother stopped doing everything for him. Today, he offered her a plate of food, and she declined.

"It's good to have you home, Thomas Jude," Sonja said to her son as he finished chewing a mouthful and used his napkin to wipe his mouth before speaking.

"Thanks mom," he replied, smiling at her. He loved her, but he missed the remarkable, vibrant woman she used to be.

"So tell me about school, your internship coming up this summer, and your social life. Are you dating?" Like Steph, TJ had not confided in his parents when he believed he met *the one* a semester ago.

"School is great, my internship will be heavy in research but I'm psyched about it!" Sonja smiled. When her son came home, she lived through him sometimes. He was curious and adventurous, just as she once was. "And, yes, I have girlfriend at school. Her name is Steph and she's beautiful and fun, and I really couldn't imagine my life without her."

"You're in love..." Sonja stated, almost with regret. She wished for this day for him and wanted to meet the girl of his dreams. *But, how embarrassing she would be as his mother? An invalid.*

"I do love her, mom," TJ stated, "and I hope you will want to meet her, soon."

"Yes, of course," Sonja spoke softly and immediately looked down at her coffee.

TJ finished eating and drank the last of the milk in the talk glass in front of him. He sat back in the patio chair in his black t-shirt, faded denim, and black flip flops on his bare feet. He wanted so badly to confide in his mother, but he knew he couldn't. He couldn't upset her like that, and his father would be irate. Still, he wanted to seek her advice.

Sonja could see in his eyes that something was bothering him. "You know, a single facial expression from you can take me back to your childhood. Like the time you broke a window practicing your swing in the front yard, or when you were sent to the principal's office for cheating on the constitution test. What's wrong, TJ? Something is on your mind, and you want to talk about it..."

Their bond was still there, but TJ had learned to protect her from pain or worry. His father had warned him of that. But, right now, TJ wasn't entirely sure that he should keep something so life-changing from his own mother. He was in trouble. His girlfriend was pregnant. His father demanded a quick fix to get rid of it. TJ wondered if maybe telling his mother could lead to her changing his father's mind. He still felt uneasy about it.

"College can stress a guy out, mom, that's all," TJ spoke, hoping he could convince her.

"I understand," Sonja said, wondering if she should push.

"How are things with you and dad?" TJ asked her.

"Okay as ever," Sonja replied, knowing her son yearned for a time he remembered when his parents couldn't keep their hands off each other. He used to roll his eyes or feign being grossed out as they held hands in public or stole kisses in front of him in the kitchen. Now, he wished to see that closeness between his parents again. It saddened him how his mother had given up on everything, even her marriage. What once appeared to be a solid, loving, and passionate marriage.

"How's your therapy, anything innovative?" TJ wanted more than anything for his mother to be stronger, in body and in mind.

"Nothing that will ever get me out if this chair, Teej." Sonja's self pity never seemed to improve. "So you know my marriage hangs by a thread and you know my body isn't getting any stronger. Now tell me what you're so afraid I cannot handle." TJ was caught off guard and didn't bother to hide it. His eyes widened and he shifted his laid back position on the chair.

"My perceptive mother," TJ commented. "The last thing I ever want to do is disappoint you."

"You couldn't," she tried to reassure him.

"I could use some advice, and probably a lot of help down the road," TJ admitted, believing there was no way Steph would ever agree to his father's solution. "What's done is done, so I'm just going to say this. And if you want to pretend I never told you, we can."

"Was that how your father reacted?" Sonja asked, already knowing her son had turned to Wade first. He did so with everything.

"Not really. He does think he has a solution," TJ sighed, "but I'm looking for a second opinion."

"Let me offer mine..." His mother's words touched him more than ever. She needed to be there for him, no matter what plagued him, just as much as he needed her right now.

"I'm sorry, mom," he began. "It's Steph. She's pregnant."

Sonja's eyes widened and her jaw dropped. This was the absolute farthest thing from her mind. This wasn't just TJ's *problem*. This was a life. This affected all of them. Direly. She looked down at her hands which had been folded on her lap. They were now shaking. Then, her eyes met her son's. He looked scared, forlorn, and lost. If there ever was a time post the accident when TJ needed her to be a mother, a real supportive mother, it was most definitely now. "A baby? When you're still finding your way as young man with a very bright future ahead?" Sonja questioned him, softly. She could hear her own heartbeat pounding in her ears.

TJ nodded his head and Sonja could see the tears welling up in his eyes. "I know I'm far from ready, mom. I told Steph it will all work out, but I don't believe my own words. I'm scared out of my mind and I don't know what to do."

Sometimes a crisis, or something as life-changing as new life, will bring people closer together. Sonja could feel the pull to her son now. It was time she was his mother again. Chair or no chair. Not having use of her legs seemed trivial at this moment, and she surprised herself feeling that way, finally. Sonja knew how to love TJ. That had never changed. But, right now, she wanted to guide him through his uncertainty.

"What you should do is take a long look at what's happening," Sonja told him. "You have a baby with your blood, your genes, and probably your big brown eyes, growing inside of a woman you say you love like you have no other. You will continue to get your education, and Steph too. And, nine months from now, I don't know about Steph's mother, but I will be ready to help you both when your baby arrives. You know I'm limited, but we will hire more help, a nanny perhaps, but I want to be present and do all I am able."

Tears were rolling down TJ's cheeks as he made his way over to his mother and dropped to his knees in front of her. He reached his arms around her and she held him. She heard him say *thank you* repeatedly and she only held him tighter. When they parted, TJ spoke first. "I'm going to need you to talk to dad for me. He wants Steph to have an abortion. He's probably already set up the appointment."

TJ sat down in a chair closer to his mother this time. "I am not too surprised. Your father likes to problem solve with quick fixes. But, honey, this is not something you should feel at ease about *getting rid of*. This is a baby, a life. I never told you this, but I had two miscarriages after you were born. I still carry that pain in my heart. I would never give up on a baby, and I do not want you to either. Do you hear me? You keep your baby. I will deal with your father."

∗∗∗

Dealing with Wade happened much sooner than Sonja had anticipated. When TJ took their plates inside to the kitchen, she thought she heard him return outside immediately. He had said he was going to call Steph, hoping she was awake already. TJ wanted her to know they had his mother's support. But, when Sonja slightly turned her wheelchair, she saw Wade approaching.

"How was breakfast with our son?" he asked her, and she immediately knew Wade had been watching them. Sonja assumed he was already at work, but since they kept separate bedrooms, she really had no idea of his schedule this morning.

"Nice," she answered.

"He told you, didn't he?" Wade asked, feeling angry with his son because he should have known better.

"Yes," Sonja replied.

"Our son will not ruin his life this way." Wade was adamant.

"It's not your choice to make," Sonja told him as he stood over her.

"No? Watch me!" Wade snapped at her. He took himself by surprise for a moment. He just didn't raise his voice to her anymore. There was nothing to discuss or even argue about. She, for ten years now, had given up on herself and on him. He, at first after the accident, had begged and pleaded with her to find her will to live again. She was his wife, and his love for her had never gone away. They had since co-existed in the same house, a mansion where they didn't even have to see each other for days if that's what they wanted, but their marriage was lost to them.

"I've already told TJ that he has my support," Sonja stated.

"For what? For the few times a year when he will come home? Is that when you're planning to play grandma?" Wade's words did not sway her.

"Why can't you be supportive?" Sonja asked him.

"I have always supported him and now I am looking out for my son's best interest. College should remain his sole focus. End of story."

"No, actually, it's just the beginning of his story. Don't rob him of this chance to become a father. Yes, the timing is all wrong but when is it ever in sync with what we want and when we need it?" Sonja was looking up at him, standing there with his arms folded across his chest. He was dressed for work in black dress pants, black slip-on polished dress shoes, and a long-sleeved light blue button-down shirt with no tie yet. There was a time when she saw him as a man who could do no wrong. But, so much had gone wrong in the last decade. She pushed him away, but they agreed to remain married for TJ's sake, who was just a boy then. Sonja knew Wade turned to other women, time and again. She didn't hate him for it anymore because she knew she could no longer be his lover. She chose not to be as she only felt like half of a woman. She once believed Wade deserved better. But, better wasn't supposed to lead him to a world of dealing and eventually becoming addicted to drugs. Yes, Sonja knew. It was a truth Wade believed he was successful at hiding from both his wife and son.

"I'll tell TJ again that we want to meet the mother of his child," Wade said, beginning to appear to back down. He always appeased Sonja, and he knew that was what she was expecting now.

"And you'll drop this craziness about talking them into having an abortion?" Sonja asked him.

"I'm the odd man out, so I have no other choice," he said to her, making direct eye contact and she acted as if she believed him.

"Thank you, Wade."

"Anything for you," he responded.

Chapter 11

For two days, Belle watched her daughter and her husband avoid each other. No words were spoken between them. When Steph took Skylar and Sammy out for ice cream, Belle used that opportunity to talk to Clint.

He was reclining on one end of the white sofa in the living room when she walked in and sat down on the chair adjacent to him. "I can remember, like it was yesterday, how my father ignored me when he found out I was pregnant." Clint looked at her. "I know you remember it, too. It was awful because his actions made me feel so ashamed."

"I just don't know what to say to her," Clint responded. "As parents we want better for our children than we had, don't we? I have high hopes for all three of them, but Steph especially."

"Because she's so much like you?" Belle asked him. "Intelligent, driven to seize the best life has to offer…"

"Having a baby in the middle of her college career isn't what's best for her," Clint stated. "She has no idea how difficult everything will get."

"No, she doesn't, but she has the same feelings as we did, and fear is dominating all of her emotions right now. It's up to us to help her. She needs us both right now, just as much as she needed us when she was born. Look at the life we gave her…we can't stop now." Belle knew she had gotten through to her husband because he fell silent and looked down.

Belle stood up, walked over to him and sat close. She put her arm on his back and rubbed it. A second later he turned to her. Belle put both of her hands on his face, wiping away a tear with her finger. "It's going to be okay," she told him. "Remember those words? You told me so twenty years ago, and you know what, it is *okay*." Before Belle could speak further, Clint met his lips with hers. He hadn't kissed her, really kissed her, like that, in a very long time. It was almost as if it was possible for their daughter's crisis to bring them back to those feelings they shared once as they were struggling to survive.

When they pulled apart, they never had a chance to say anything to each other as car doors were heard slamming shut outside and their children were back home.

MIRROR IMAGE

All three of them walked into the house, talking and laughing and eating their ice cream. Belle watched as Steph carried a large chocolate milkshake and a vanilla ice cream cone in both of her hands. She walked up to Clint and handed him the milkshake. "Here, dad. I know this is your favorite."

Clint took the milkshake from his daughter and immediately set it down on the table next to him. He never said a word as he stood up, directly in front of Steph. Belle could see the tears back in his eyes as Steph looked up at him wide-eyed. He was a few inches taller than her five-seven frame. Clint opened his arms and Steph fell into them. The other two children were watching closely as they already knew their sister was going to have a baby. Steph started to cry and Clint put his hand on the back of her head of long, dark hair as he held her against his chest. "It's going to be okay," they all heard him say, and everyone in that room, in their family, believed him.

***

Belle was still packing her suitcase after everyone was in bed. She and Steph were planning to leave in the morning for the ten-hour drive to Silver Spring, Maryland. Steph had agreed to meet TJ's parents after he reassured her that his dad was no longer pushing for them to abort the baby. Belle, tagging along for the trip, was her idea. At first, Steph balked and told her it would be awkward because she was planning to stay with TJ, and where would that leave her? Belle giggled and told her she would stay at a nearby hotel because she only wanted to meet TJ and his parents, and especially accompany Steph during her long commute to Silver Spring.

All of her clothes, shoes, and most of her toiletries were tucked neatly into medium-size suitcase of the set of five she and Clint shared. Their bedroom was dimly lit by just one lamp near the door. Belle was now on her knees at the foot-end of their bed. They had a storage chest, with a padded, pastel plaid, cushion on top, and inside they kept miscellaneous things like ball caps for Clint, a large brimmed straw hat that Belle wore in the sun. Right now, Belle was feeling her way through the chest to find a small, black case with a combination code. She reached for it, held it in her hands, and then placed it down on the carpet in front of her. It was almost too dark to see, but she managed to put their anniversary date as the number combination on the lock and it opened.

Clint had a license to conceal and carry a handgun. *It was just for their safety*, he told her, *and I really only want a gun for protection in the house. We will keep it in our bedroom, in our cedar chest at the foot of the bed.* Belle had never held it before, much less handled or loaded it. But, she had observed Clint. She wasn't at all timid about taking the gun out of the case and tucking it deep inside her suitcase, underneath her underwear. She went back to the case to retrieve an entire box of ammunition. She hadn't checked to see if the gun was already loaded, and she didn't want to rattle the bullets in that small box and risk waking Clint. So, the entire box of one hundred rounds also was tucked beneath her delicates at the base of her suitcase.

"What are you doing? Still packing?" Clint spoke with his voice low in the dark, and Belle felt startled.

"Um, yes, just about done," she replied. She left her suitcase on the floor. She closed the lid, but did not zip it. She would need to add her toothbrush and makeup in the morning. Belle turned off the lamp by their closed bedroom door, and walked through the dark to their bed. She was already wearing her white t-shirt, no bra, and this time no panties because she had packed all of her favorites, and the rest needed to be laundered. She never thought about it again as she slipped into bed and pulled up the covers to her chest. Clint rolled and she expected a quick goodnight kiss, *see you in the morning, love you*.

His kiss was longer, his hands were moving up her leg and then he found her with no panties. She giggled a little and attempted to explain that all of them were packed, but his fingers touching her nearly took her breath. She tightened and then relaxed her legs, spreading them, enticing her husband to do more.

This was so out of the ordinary for them. They rarely touched. Life was too busy. The passion in their late thirties wasn't what it used to be. Belle was reacting to him. Kissing him back. Reaching into his red boxer shorts to feel his body's response to her. Her t-shirt was up, her husband's mouth had found the nipple of her right breast, the one closest to him as he kept his fingers between her legs and then moved inside of her. She arched her back, rocked her body. Their bed frame began to squeak. Clint found her clitoris and moved his finger slowly back and forth. She couldn't take it anymore. She placed her hand on top of his and forced an in sync faster motion. Clint obliged and his wife climaxed on his fingers. He straddled her quickly in their dark bedroom and plunged inside of her. He paid no mind to their squeaky bed frame as he came inside of her after only six or eight hard and fast thrusts.

Afterward, they laid beside each other, not speaking. Sometimes they were too set in the routine of life. Twenty years together. Three children. Jobs. Busy days and nights. If only they could relearn how to put each other first again. Tonight, just maybe, was a good start.

✲✲✲

Wade was lying flat on his back on the bed he slept in alone in the west wing of the mansion. His wife's bedroom was clear on the other side of their massive home. She had kept the bedroom they shared in the east wing before her accident. Right now, Wade was not thinking of his wife as he laid on top of the cherry red duvet, wearing only his black silk pajama bottoms, low on his waist. He closed his eyes, the rush was over, and this was such a relaxed state for him. He never snorted more, or less, he had definitely found his balance. Wade was in total control. Morning and night. Those were the only two times when his body needed heroin. He believed he had himself trained. He knew he should have been more thorough with Gabi. Kept a better, watchful eye on her as she became more comfortable and in control of it. It was too dangerous how he just gave it to her when she could not yet handle it. He missed her. Not a day went by where he didn't feel regret. He never let it consume him, though. That was not Wade Morgan. He was a man in control of his life. The only time he had ever felt like he was spiraling was the day his wife was hit by a truck while walking on a sidewalk, close to her office downtown.

He remembered entering that hospital room, seeing her body broken, hearing the doctor tell them she would never walk again. *Permanent paralysis from the waist down. His sweet Sonja should have died that day,* Wade thought time and again, *because she had been lost to him and their son ever since.* And now, she was encouraging their son to have this baby with his girlfriend. She suddenly had an opinion and wanted to guide their son. Wade had already hired the physician. And he was prepared to make a house call as soon as Wade gave him the word. *Just a matter of days and my son can resume his path to a successful future,* Wade thought to himself as he drifted off to sleep, still lying at the foot of the bed and on top of the cherry red duvet.

Chapter 12

Five hours into their trip, Belle had done all of the driving as Steph was either on her cell phone or asleep. She complained about feeling queasy, and Belle told her she had packed some dry cereal and crackers for her. Before she attempted to eat any of it, Steph just laid her head back against the passenger seat and closed her eyes.

This trip had given Belle some time to think. As she put miles and miles between her and home, she became more unlike herself. Her thoughts were consumed of Gabi. She felt such rage when she thought of her being *dead*, and exactly how she had lost her life. This man, this Wade Morgan, was to blame.

Belle felt guilty not being honest with her husband and her daughter when she put the pieces together about Wade Morgan. But, she knew she had to take care of this herself. Steph had not known what city in Maryland her aunt was planning to relocate to, and Clint had never paid any attention. Five more hours on the road, and Belle would introduce herself to the man who she believed *killed* her twin sister.

✳✳✳

After only stopping for two bathroom breaks and to eat lunch, Belle and Steph arrived in Silver Spring at seven o'clock that evening. "I'm nervous about meeting them," Steph admitted to her mother as she pulled down the visor in front of her to look in the small mirror. She had already reapplied her makeup as Belle drove, and changed her hairstyle twice. She had finally decided on a French braid that she did herself.

"You're bound to be," Belle said, reading the street signs in front of her and listening to the annoying GPS narrator. "Just remember, TJ loves you. His parents will too, I'm sure of it." Steph smiled at her mother and wished they were at TJ's home already. She just wanted to get this first meeting over with. Belle, on the other hand, didn't feel the slightest bit nervous. She did, however, feel prepared.

On the outside of the gated subdivision, Belle and Steph looked at each other. They felt as if they were entering a tour of the homes of the rich and famous. "Any idea what his parents do for a living?" Belle asked Steph, knowing there was no possible way she was aware that TJ's father owned a fashion business. She would have brought that up and mentioned Gabi and her clothing line, for sure. It should have amazed Belle how little Steph seemed to know about the father of her child's background. But, she was in her daughter's place once too. She once dated Clint and just enjoyed his company. Parents, careers, extended family, none of that was on their minds or a part of their conversations.

"Um, well, his mom was a licensed clinical worker before the accident, and his dad owns his own corporation," Steph stated.

"That's right, that's a shame about his mother. Why doesn't she still practice?" Belle asked.

"TJ said she's not well. Her mind always seems to be somewhere else," Steph stated.

Belle nodded her head. They drove entirely through the subdivision and made a left hand turn onto a narrow, windy road that led them deeper into the countryside than Belle had expected. Two and half miles down the road, Belle could see the house, and she wondered what exactly they were about to walk into as she parked in the massive circle drive area in front of a residence which looked like something straight out of a Hollywood movie.

The brick was an ivory color and the pillars in front of the house were an identical match. There wasn't much color to that massive home, as everything from the window trim to the shutters and the even the front door all blended. It was ritzy and Belle admired it as she and Steph stepped up to the front door. "Here goes nothing," Steph said, and Belle smiled at her. She then said to her daughter what she'd always said when she was embarking on something new in her young life. "Chin up, and never forget how easy you are to love."

TJ opened the door just seconds after Steph pushed her finger to the fancy bell which looked like a button embedded into a bronzed, Celtic knot. "Steph," Belle heard this young man say her daughter's name. He was every bit of six-foot with dark hair, brown eyes, and an olive skin tone much like Steph's. Belle watched the two of them embrace and she saw TJ momentarily close his eyes when he had her daughter in his arms. *So genuine*, Belle thought, as she watched two young adults relish a moment.

"TJ, this is my mom, Isabelle," Steph said, introducing her. TJ had known she was coming along and he also prepared his mother who was waiting for all of them now.

"It's a pleasure, ma'am" TJ said, offering his hand and Belle took it.

"Thank you, and you can call me, Belle," she told him, with a sweet smile.

TJ led the way inside and when they reached the living room, he walked them all the way through it. "My mother is outside on the patio terrace," he told them. "She loves the evening air this time of year." Belle nodded her head and wondered what kind of woman she was about to meet. Steph had only known a few details about her, most of it vague.

The view from the patio terrace, as TJ had called it, was breathtaking. The stamped concrete, the landscaping, the May flowers in full bloom, and the immense swimming pool down below. Belle felt as if she could stare at that blue water circulating in a clockwise motion until the sun set.

Steph and TJ were close and holding hands as they walked toward his mother. Sonja heard them coming from behind, and Belle watched her turn her wheelchair to them. She looked frail, but her arms were obviously strong enough to move herself.

Belle stood back, and watched the scene. "Mom, this is Steph, the woman I love." TJ's words brought a smile to each of their faces. Steph, because TJ always had the perfect words. Sonja, because this young woman made her son happy. And, Belle, because what mother would not beam knowing her daughter had found true love.

Steph took one step closer to Sonja in her wheelchair. TJ had forewarned her, during one of their text conversations earlier today, how she should not look at his mother with pity in her eyes. *Greet her and treat her like a whole person.* No one did that anymore, and TJ wanted that from Steph, more than anything. His father treated her like fragile glass. Her therapists even gave in when she gave up. But, not TJ. He promised himself he would never look at his mother as anything less than she was before the accident. He still had hope for her to, one day, regain that light in her eyes and a zest for life he once fed off of as a child. His mother was once fun and exciting and TJ was so much like her.

"It's so good to meet you, Mrs. Morgan," Steph said, offering her hand, and Sonja immediately lifted her hand to receive it.

"Likewise, my dear," Sonja spoke with a strong voice, and TJ smiled at her. "Given the circumstances, I want you to know my home is your home from this day on. The baby you are carrying is wanted and will be loved."

Steph could have wrapped her arms around the woman in front of her, but she contained what would have been perceived as a ridiculous outburst, considering they were strangers. Steph smiled and thanked her, sincerely.

"Mom, I'd also like you to meet Belle, Steph's mother," TJ turned around and motioned for Belle to come closer.

Belle walked slowly up to the woman in the wheelchair and offered her hand. "What an interesting way to meet, knowing we already share such a gift. A grandchild," Belle said, smiling as Sonja took her hand and held it with one of hers and then both.

She gently sandwiched Belle's hand in between hers, and spoke in a teasing manner. "We are both entirely too young to be called *Grandma*, so we must put our heads together to come up with a more chic name." They all giggled and TJ was in awe of what was happening in front of him. His mother was being affectionate, loving, and she was exemplifying her clever wit again.

After much small talk was shared sitting at the patio table under the pergola, TJ and Steph went into the house to unpack her things. Steph assumed she would be sharing TJ's bedroom. She wanted to. Considering they had already conceived a baby, it seemed trivial to even give a second thought.

The silence was short-lived between the two women as the night sky began to darken. Sonja tugged at the pink sweater draped over her shoulders when the wind picked up. The air was still warm and Belle had been wearing faded flared denim, black flip flops and a black linen oxford shirt, with the sleeves rolled up to her elbows. She was comfortable in the night air, but she wondered about Sonja, who was dressed in gray yoga pants and a white thermal Henley. Belle also noticed that she was wearing thick white socks on her feet. "If you want to go inside, I can show you to your room," Sonja offered, kindly.

"Oh, I was planning to stay at a local hotel or inn," Belle explained. "This is Steph's time with your family. She was invited here, and I don't want to impose."

"Nonsense, Belle," Sonja spoke and hearing her say her name felt nice for Belle. Like it was coming from an old friend. "This place could be a hotel. I had the maid get a room ready just for you...and quite frankly I think your daughter may feel more comfortable having you close. I mean, can you imagine as a young girl how it would feel to meet your boyfriend's parents for the first time when everyone knows you're carrying a baby?"

Belle nodded her head in agreement, "Actually, I can. For me, it was the third meeting with *his* parents. I got pregnant with Steph at nineteen."

"Ahh, that explains your understanding for your

daughter. TJ has told me how supportive you have been." Sonja felt the same connection to Belle. She could not remember the last time she had spoken to another woman as a girlfriend. This was a therapy like no other.

"Well I couldn't be anything else, having been there, too." Belle smiled and took a sip from the glass of iced water with lemon that TJ had brought her from the kitchen earlier when Sonja requested a hot tea.

"May I ask what you do for a living?" Sonja inquired.

"I am a guidance counselor at a junior high school," Belle told her.

"I see," Sonja nodded. "I used to be, um, before my accident when Teej was eleven years old, a licensed clinical social worker. You just seem so easy to talk to. I believed instantly that your occupation was some form of communication. You naturally put people at ease."

"Well, thank you," Belle told her. "Kids are awkward at that level and I certainly hope I am successful at making them feel at ease. You said you were licensed in clinical social work, do you miss practicing?"

"All the time," Sonja admitted, "but look at me. I could never go back. Who would take me seriously from this chair?" This was the first time tonight that Sonja demonstrated even an inkling of self pity, and Belle did feel sorry for her. But, she didn't let it show.

"With beauty and intelligence like yours, only a fool would not look past your handicap. I apologize if my word use offends you," Belle was quick to add, "but I'm simply stating what I see. You do have physical limitations, yes, but why let what your legs cannot do barricade anything else you could be doing with your life? You used to heal people, mind, body, and soul, I assume. That's a gift."

Sonja took a deep breath, and then smiled. She felt like tearing up, but she also felt strong. "I have been slowly dying for the past decade. No doctors or therapists have ever said to me what you just said. Or, maybe they have, and I just have not heard them. Thank you for your sincerity and honesty, but most of all, for your encouragement."

Inside of the house, TJ and Steph were wrapped in each other's arms in his bed. They could hardly wait to make love to each other and that's exactly what they had done as soon as they closed and locked the door behind them.

"I cannot believe our mothers are getting along like life-long girlfriends on the patio terrace and you and I are naked two stories up," Steph giggled.

"I'm not sure which part of what you just said makes me happier," TJ confessed. "My mother hasn't been so lively and pleasant in years. And, having you naked beside me is blissful." TJ kissed her long and hard and Steph responded with everything she had. She loved him and despite the fact that their timing was terrible, she did want to have his baby.

***

Steph and TJ were dressed again and downstairs on the main level of the house in the kitchen. They were hungry and TJ was leaning forward with his head in the refrigerator as he was naming off a few food choices for them to eat. Steph was seated on the corner of the L-shaped granite-top island when she saw him walk in. His build was exactly like TJ's, even his height. His blond hair was wavy and styled perfectly on his head. He was dressed to the nines in a dark suit and yellow tie.

"Hello," Wade spoke, and TJ backed out of the refrigerator as Steph stood up from the stool she had been sitting on. "No, please, no need to stand up on my account. Make yourself at home. I'm Thomas Jude's father." Steph found it funny to hear TJ's full name pronounced, and she replied, *I'm Stephanie Madden*, and then Wade took her hand in his.

"You're a beautiful girl, Stephanie," Wade complimented her.

"Thank you," Steph felt her cheeks flush, and TJ was now standing beside her. He knew she felt intimidated by his father. Wade Morgan had that affect on everyone.

"Did you make the long road trip without issues?" Wade asked, and TJ recalled only telling his mother that Steph's mother was coming along.

"Yes, my mother did most of the driving," Steph said, thinking how Belle did all of the driving, but she didn't want to appear to be too young to handle it.

"Oh, so your mother is in town?" Wade asked, surprised, and not liking the feeling of having pertinent information kept from him. He had specific plans for this girl's stay at their home. *And her mother would definitely get in the way.*

"Yes, she will be staying at a hotel," Steph started to say, and that's when the French doors leading into the kitchen opened and Sonja wheeled herself inside. It was now dark outside and Wade could see a woman, standing back, holding the door while his wife entered the house.

"Your mother will be staying with us, and I will not accept a refusal," Sonja informed all of three of them standing near the island in the kitchen. TJ and Steph nodded their heads in unison. They were both relieved and excited to know their mothers had become fast friends.

"I see," Wade spoke to Sonja as he took steps to reach the doorway. Sonja rolled past him, practically ignoring his presence which wasn't anything out of the ordinary, but this time Wade was more concerned about meeting the woman who was bound to get in the way with his plans for Stephanie Madden.

Belle knew exactly what she was doing when she stayed back, in the dark of night, and then she gradually stepped into the light which lit up the kitchen doorway like a stage. And on center stage she was, and her performance was flawless as she made sure Wade took in the sight of her face before she spoke. Belle knew damn well she looked exactly like her twin sister, and the look that registered on Wade's face was only being seen by her. His back was to the rest of them in the kitchen as Belle watched his eyes widen, his expression fall, and the color drain from his face.

"Hello, Wade, right? I'm Belle Madden. It's nice to finally meet you." Both TJ and Steph had Sonja's attention, as the three of them were discussing ordering either a late-night pizza or

Chinese food. No one paid any mind to what was happening in the open doorway of the kitchen. The young adults were hungry and Sonja wanted to spend more time with Belle. The idea of a late dinner appealed to all three of them.

Wade's arms remained at his sides. He knew Gabi Lange had a twin sister, he had seen Belle before, at the funeral home. But, that was quick as he passed through the receiving line not wanting to be noticed then. He knew TJ's pregnant girlfriend was from Maine. The odds of that girl being Gabi's niece were incredibly ridiculous. And the fact that Gabi's twin sister was staring at him right now as if she knew everything had sent eerie and frightening chills all throughout his body. A man always in control was caught off guard at this moment like never before. He did manage to reach out his hand and receive Belle's.

He took a deep breath. He could hear the thump of his own heart inside of his ears. His forehead was beading with perspiration. He felt like he needed a fix, right there and now. He took a second deep and longer breath, and told himself that his secret was safe. This woman could not have known who he was. *Could she?*

Chapter 13

Small talk carried them all through sharing pizza as they gathered around the L-shaped island for another hour and a half. TJ and Steph seemed so happy to be together again. Belle and Sonja continued to connect and relate to each other in ways that awed them both. Wade, especially, could not believe the effect Belle had on his wife. Sonja was no longer sad and withdrawn. She was, however, her distant, cold self with him. And Belle noticed immediately. There was very little eye contact shared and it appeared as if the harder Wade tried, the more Sonja pulled away from him.

It was close to eleven-thirty when TJ and Steph excused themselves, saying they were tired. Belle and Sonja both wished them a good night, and when they left the kitchen the two women acted as if Wade wasn't even there. "Remember being young and in love? Those excuses we made to be alone? We were never tired," Sonja was giggling as she spoke and Belle joined her. "I only wish the two of them had more time for each other, you know, before becoming parents," Sonja spoke honestly. "A baby will change everything." She glanced at Wade and he was looking at her too. He hadn't wanted to have children, but when Sonja became pregnant and TJ was born, Wade was an incredible father. And still was in so many ways.

"I agree," Belle said, thinking how she and Clint's relationship had changed with each passing year.

Wade interrupted before Belle could say more. "Excuse me while I also call it a night." He walked over to Sonja, and Belle watched them closely. "Good night, my love," he said kissing her on top of her head and resting his hand on her shoulder. Sonja only reached up to pat his hand and then quickly removed her hand from his. "Don't stay up too late, it's already past your bedtime. And, be careful, transitioning into bed." Belle realized then how they must have separate bedrooms. She fumed a little inside just thinking how he had cheated on Sonja. One of his lovers had been Gabi. "Belle, again, it was a pleasure." Wade never reached for her hand and Belle never offered anything more than saying, "Yes, likewise." She gave him direct eye contact and he again felt chills seep through this body. He could hardly handle to look at her, yet he wanted to stare. She was Gabi all over again, only her body's frame was slightly thicker.

When Wade left the room, Belle spoke first. "Your husband implied that you may need help getting into bed? Is there something I can do?" Belle wondered if there was hired help for Sonja at nighttime.

"Heavens no, I've been helping myself from this chair to my bed for years. I've only fallen a few times," Sonja giggled while Belle covered her own mouth in surprise with her hand. "No harm done," Sonja added, and Belle giggled with her.

"Can I be honest with you about something?" Sonja asked as she and Belle were getting ready to leave the kitchen, and the mess. Apparently the maid would get it in the morning before breakfast, Belle learned.

"Of course," Belle said, facing Sonja in her wheelchair.

"I am an extremely sad and lonely person," Sonja spoke so seriously, and Belle felt drawn to her. "I knew, today, I had to pull out of that, for my son's sake. I swore to myself that I would be pleasant and warm with Steph. And, I had no idea what to expect meeting her mother. I didn't want to like you, I don't like anyone anymore." Sonja paused as Belle couldn't help but think how sad her life was. Her fortune, her home had to be the envy of many, but her life not so much. "But, here you are, and here I am, and I just feel so different. Happy again? Alive? Maybe. Just know that I think you are an amazing person and I love knowing your daughter will be the mother of my grandbaby. Our grandbaby."

Both of the women smiled so sincerely at each other, and then Belle reached for Sonja's hands. This was suddenly difficult for Belle. Sonja had been honest with her, but she in turn was not. Belle was hiding so much. *She knew Wade and her*

MIRROR IMAGE

sister had an affair. He had hired her to work for his fashion corporation. He had turned her to drugs. He was the reason Gabi died. Belle wondered how she could possibly nurture this newfound friendship between her and Sonja when it was based on a lie. A part of Belle just wanted to get the hell out of there, and never look back. But, she couldn't. She had Steph, and the baby, to think about.

"I think you're the amazing one," Belle told her as she released her hands from holding Sonja's, leaned closer, hugged her tightly, and wished her good night.

✶✶✶

In the room that Sonja had directed her to, Belle began to unpack a few items from her suitcase. At the bottom, she found Clint's handgun. *What exactly was she going to do with that? Had she really thought she could use it? Wade Morgan deserved to pay for what he did to her sister. But, violence? An eye for an eye?* Just in case, Belle carefully and effectively loaded the gun in her hands. If anything, she just wanted to be prepared, because she did not trust Wade Morgan.

Two doors down, Wade was pacing the floor of his bedroom. He needed a fix, and that would come in a few minutes as he prepared to sleep. Now, he contemplated what to do with Belle when the physician he hired would make a house call tomorrow. Wade thought about using Sonja's newfound friendship with Belle to keep both of them occupied. *It could work,* he thought. And then he thought of how beautiful she was. Just like Gabi. Only Belle, very much unlike her twin sister, had seemed oblivious to her beauty. Wade had not loved another woman since Sonja. The accident had changed her and she was lost to him afterward. It was Gabi, though, who had only just begun to capture his heart. He was consumed with guilt for introducing her to heroin when he wasn't certain if she could handle the danger. *His life and guilt.* My, how it had gone hand in hand for too many years.

In his bare feet and black silk pajama bottoms hanging low on his hips, Wade bent forward over the desk against the wall. The white powdery substance was already in place on the tiny, squared mirror. He inhaled the exact same amount every night. It always took two and a half nasal draw-ins for Wade to clear the mirror of the substance. After nearly a decade, he was skilled, as if that was something to be proud of. Within minutes, the heroin always put him in the most calm state and then he would fall asleep. Tonight, he laid on his bed and closed his eyes. His body was relaxed but his mind was still reeling.

✳ ✳ ✳

Belle was sitting up in bed, with a pillow propped up against the headboard to cushion her back. After only a few hours of sleep in a strange place, she was responding to multiple texts from Clint. *How is it there? Give me your opinion on TJ and his parents. Are you and Steph still planning to drive home tomorrow? The kids miss you.*

Belle told him their daughter's boyfriend appears to be a wonderful young man. She added that his mother already feels like a friend. She left out any details about Wade Morgan, only saying she had not spent much time with TJ's father yet. She told Clint that she also missed the kids, and him, and hoped to leave for home tomorrow, as planned. Belle wondered if Steph would be ready to leave TJ, but she had been adamant about this trip being for the purpose of meeting the parents and to discuss the baby on the way.

That topic was exactly what TJ and Steph were discussing over breakfast with Wade when Belle walked into the kitchen. Any kind of breakfast food imaginable had been prepared by the chef, Belle assumed, as she came into the kitchen, taking in the aroma of food and eyeing her company. TJ and Steph were dressed in sweats and t-shirts. TJ was wearing a baseball cap and Steph had her long dark hair pulled up in a messy knot on top of her head. Wade was in faded jeans, brown loafers, sans socks, and a navy blue half-zip pullover. Belle wondered what his plans were today. She had hoped he would be working so she could enjoy the kids and Sonja without Wade's awkward presence. She had thought long and hard last night about her feelings for him. She hated him and didn't even know him. She, from six hundred miles away, had thought she could put a bullet in him for taking her sister away from her. But, in reality, Belle was a wife, and mother, and a straight arrow. She was not a violent person. And, despite her pain now and the craziness he briefly brought into Gabi's life before her untimely death, Belle knew this man meant something to her daughter's boyfriend and he also would become a grandparent when Belle would.

Belle, in a white casual ankle-length broomstick skirt with white canvas Toms on her feet and a long-sleeved linen lilac oxford shirt, poured herself a cup of coffee after greeting them all *good morning* at once. "I'm glad you're joining us,"

Wade spoke to Belle as she sat down at the table directly across from him while TJ was at her left and Steph at her right. "There's something we've been discussing and wish to run it by you." Belle sipped her hot coffee slowly, holding the clear glass mug with both of her hands, as Wade continued to speak.

"Your plans to leave tomorrow are completely understandable to me, as I know you have a husband and Steph's younger siblings to get home to. TJ has another week and a half here at home before he begins his summer internship back in Maine. We were hoping you would agree to allow Steph to stay with us and then she can return to Maine with TJ when he goes back to the university." Wade's idea, or maybe it was TJ and Steph's idea, sounded reasonable. *If it had been any other family.* Belle did not trust Wade, and because she had not been honest with her daughter about him, Steph would not know to keep her guard up around him.

"I see," Belle began. "I do have to get back to my family, and we really didn't plan very well for Steph to stay here. I mean, her clothes, she's only packed for a few days…"

"Mom, I'm like you, I always over pack. I'll be fine," Steph told her, and TJ added, "We'll go shopping for whatever else she needs." The smiles on their faces touched Belle. They were twenty years old, but still like children, or at least teenagers, in so many ways. This wasn't an extended sleepover. This was real life. Belle liked this young man in Steph's world, and she hoped he would be true to his word as Clint was two decades ago when they had a baby on the way.

"I will consider agreeing to this," Belle spoke to both Steph and TJ, "but, first, I would like to speak to your father alone." TJ looked surprised and Steph seemed confused. Both TJ and Steph carried their breakfast plates and drink glasses with them out onto the patio terrace. Steph didn't look back, she just trusted her mom knew what she was doing as Belle wondered what in the world she was getting herself into.

Wade was sitting across from her. His neatly combed blond hair still looked wet from the shower. He took his fork and poked a grape on his breakfast plate, brought it to his mouth and ate it. And then he looked at Belle. She noticed his eyes looked tired, and the whites appeared pinkish red. She flashed back momentarily in her mind to the night she had dinner, her last meal, with Gabi. Her eyes looked the same then.

"So you want to speak to me alone?" Wade asked, wondering why they were sitting in silence. He still had a difficult time looking at her without thinking of Gabi.

"I do," Belle said, wondering if Sonja was also outside on the patio terrace already or if she had been sleeping in.

It was as if Wade was reading her mind when he spoke again. "My wife's physical therapist is with her upstairs now, if you wish to wait for her to talk this over?" Wade suggested, hoping her mind was not made up, or possibly Sonja could influence her to allow her daughter to stay. Wade knew if Belle wasn't around, he would be able to ensure that Steph met with the physician and his son's future would no longer be tarnished.

"What I have to say can be said without Sonja," Belle began. "You see, I know who you are. I see they way you look at me, struggling not to see *her*." Wade set his fork down slowly on the edge of his plate. This woman, confronting him like this, was something he was expecting and dreading at the same time.

He listened as Belle held nothing back. "I know you hired my sister, I know you bedded my sister, and I know you killed my sister." Belle felt her insides quiver, but she remained calm and collective on the exterior.

Wade put both of his hands on the tabletop in front of him. He had pushed his plate forward and then stood up. He walked over and sat down in the chair Steph had been sitting on, to the right of Belle. "First of all," he kept his voice low, "I did hire Gabi," hearing him say her name infuriated her, "and I know she would have achieved great things with her line, working for me. As for you, accusing me of cheating on my wife, I deny that. And taking someone's life? Your sister OD'd when she was alone in her apartment. The autopsy and police investigation report said as much, and then the case was closed." Wade suddenly appeared overconfident and Belle didn't like him sitting so close to her.

"I know what the reports say," Belle replied, not taking her eyes off of his. "I also know my sister never touched illegal drugs until she met you. You introduced her to your *sick* way of life, and she died because of it."

"I'm going to stand up from this table and offer you some breakfast to go with that coffee you're drinking in my kitchen," Wade said to her. "You may accept it, or decline, that's your prerogative. You're a guest in my home, and your daughter is carrying my son's baby. I suggest you and I come to some sort of understanding if we are all going to make this work, for our children. You have some nerve to accuse me of adultery *and* murder when you don't know all of the facts. I *loved* your sister," Wade suddenly whispered, and Belle's eyes widened, "and I wish I had died instead of her." His bloodshot eyes were teary as he moved from the kitchen table.

Belle contemplated stopping him as he had already walked past the L-shaped granite-topped island, and moved toward the doorway. He looked forlorn when he left, and Belle wondered if he was playing her. It was possible he could be a master of deceit. He was a drug addict, and a dealer. There was no way she could leave her daughter in this house, it was dangerous. And stupid, considering what she knew.

Chapter 14

Belle was staring at the coffee in her clear glass mug. She needed to get Steph alone to talk. She had to tell her the truth about Wade. She wanted her to have her guard up around that man. Belle realized she should have told Steph sooner and now she felt uneasy about keeping a secret so dire.

The worry must have shown on her face as Sonja made her way into the kitchen and quietly watched Belle for a moment. "Is everything alright?" Sonja asked, feeling like she may be prying.

Belle looked up quickly and then she felt at ease to see Sonja. "Oh, I hope so. I'm just concerned about Steph." That was partially the truth.

Sonja made her way to the table in her wheelchair. She was wearing a coral sweatsuit today with those thick white socks on her feet again, and her long dark hair was pulled back into a low ponytail. "I know, I'm worried too. It's not going to be easy for our kids." Belle nodded in agreement. *Had Sonja known exactly what kind of man her husband was? And, if not, was it really Belle's place to tell her?*

"Have you had more than just coffee for breakfast?" Sonja asked her.

"No, I guess I'm not really that hungry," Belle told her. "The kids and your husband told me already this morning that Steph may stay here with TJ until he goes back to Maine for his internship in almost two weeks."

"You don't want to leave her?" Sonja asked, admiring Belle for being overprotective. She used to be that way with TJ, before the accident, when everything mattered to her.

"I don't trust your husband," Belle spoke bluntly and honestly and she wondered if she should take back what she said. It seemed too late to make an excuse now. And she wasn't sure if she wanted to. Sonja already felt like her friend.

"Has he done something?" Sonja asked, not surprised nor offended by Belle's words.

"You know how this world can seem really small sometimes?" Belle began. "Here you are living in Maryland and I'm more than six hundred miles away. Our children ended up going to the same University, meeting, falling in love, and even before they told us they had gotten pregnant, our families were intertwined." Sonja listened carefully, but she was not entirely following Belle. She remained silent as Belle continued to explain her story. "I had a twin sister. She was my world, my best friend for thirty-nine years. She died six weeks ago…"

When Belle paused, Sonja brought her hand to her mouth, and she said, "Oh dear…how?"

"That's a question I will dread answering for the rest of my life," Belle replied. "Gabi and I were identical twins, but I carried at least twenty extra pounds." Belle smirked and Sonja shook her head, believing it was nonsense if Belle was implying she was overweight. Sonja would have given anything to complain about a little weight gain. She had bigger things to sulk about. "Gabi was, to me, the perfect one. She didn't get pregnant at nineteen. She finished college on time and without delay she kicked off her career in fashion." Sonja immediately thought of Wade the founder and CEO of Morgan Fashion, Inc. "She was a designer, with her own brand name, *Gabi*. Six weeks ago, my sister was prepared to make a career move, here, to Maryland. I didn't know as many of the details as I now wished I had, but your husband hired her."

Sonja shifted her upper body weight in her wheelchair. She looked uncomfortable, but Belle never noticed as she felt so nervous at this moment, knowing she was risking her new-found friendship with Sonja. She did not want to cause Sonja any additional pain. But, it already was blatantly obvious to Belle that Sonja and Wade were estranged living in the same house.

"Sonja," Belle spoke gently, "Gabi told me she was involved with Wade." Sonja never moved her eyes off of Belle. She didn't look taken aback, or angry. Her face, in fact, showed very little emotion.

"I want to hear the rest of your story," Sonja told her, as she knew there was more. Belle obliged.

"I had dinner with my sister the night she died. I thought I was seeing exhaustion and apprehension on her face, in her mannerisms. I blamed it all on the move, the life change she was embarking on. I told her goodbye in the parking lot of the restaurant. I went home and got ready for bed. And then I knew something was wrong. I could feel that she needed me," Belle sighed. She had not repeated this story to anyone. "When I got to her, it was too late. She was slumped over in the middle of her living room floor. I could see what happened, but I didn't believe it. They told me it was a drug overdose. My sister never did drugs. But, apparently she was a rookie, as your husband had just introduced her to his world." Belle looked away for a moment and then she gradually set her eyes back on Sonja.

Sonja was calm, completely at ease, and she spoke instantly. "I am so sorry for your loss. It sounds as if your sister was reeled into a world she had no idea the dangers of."

"Thank you, and your words are exact. That wasn't Gabi, and I feel as if I will spend the rest of my life defending her memory because of how she left this world. I hope you know what it means to me to know you understand that's not who she was. I, um, I realize it has to be difficult for you to know she was your husband's mistress. I don't even know if Gabi knew he was married. Honestly, I don't."

"No need to agonize over that detail," Sonja reassured her. "Your sister wasn't the first and will not be the last…"

"Can I ask you something?" Belle spoke.

"I think, considering the depth of this conversation, you and I are open to discuss anything." Sonja smiled and Belle reached for her hand. She squeezed it gently, and then let go again.

"Why do you stay with him? The drugs? The women? It's not a life you deserve." Belle was careful not to overstep, but she wanted to be honest. She believed Sonja deserved more.

"Look at me," Sonja said, taking her hands and slapping them in sync on top of her own thighs. "I do not feel that. I feel nothing in my legs…and over time, my heart became the same way. Lifeless."

Belle wasn't sure how to respond to those words, so she spoke from *her* heart. "I wish so much was different for you. I hope you know that."

Sonja smiled again, such a warm smile. She truly cared about this woman who had just come into her life, but she wondered why she was really there now. "Why did you come here?"

"To support my daughter, first and foremost," Belle answered, honestly, "and to meet the man, face to face, who took my sister away from me. Sonja, I'm not a violent person but a part of me wants him to suffer."

"I understand," Sonja replied. "but you will not be able to get ahead of him. He is a master at what he does. The drugs.

The persuasive demeanor. My accident not only changed me forever, but him as well. Believe it or not, I'd rather be me in this chair than him. I, at least, still have my soul. I control my emotions, and so what if I'm sad or in pain most of the time, at least I'm not dependent on a drug that has become me."

"Does he know that you are aware of *everything*?" Belle asked her.

"We've never discussed it. I've never confronted him. Wade and I have always been able to read each other in an uncanny sense. I don't care how many women he beds. I know I'll never be his lover again. I do care that your sister was a victim, but as for Wade's drug use and who he pulls into his web, that's not my concern. If, however, he were to bring my son into that circle, he would not live to see tomorrow. And he knows that, even though that threat has remained unspoken. And before you ask, I will tell you, TJ knows. He knows because I told him. I wanted to be the one he heard the truth from. His father, the fashion mogul, earns half of his millions on drug deals. That is why my son has chosen a path outside of fashion. I didn't have to ask him to. It was just understood."

"So you have kept Wade out of prison for your son?" Belle believed Sonja had the power and could obtain the proof to take away her husband's freedom.

"What we don't do for our children…" Sonja responded, and Belle slowly nodded, wholeheartedly. Both women would kill for their children.

Chapter 15

Belle and Sonja were briefly interrupted during their heartfelt conversation which, despite Belle's fear, had brought them even closer. TJ walked through the kitchen, put his and Steph's breakfast dishes on the countertop. He told his mother and Belle that he was going to take a shower, while Steph continued to enjoy the morning sun and the view by the swimming pool.

But, outside, she wasn't alone. Wade had made his way down the path of stepping stones in the landscape rock to get to her. He had startled her for a moment, but then she relaxed when he began to tell her about a clubhouse, as TJ used to call it when he was a boy, on the grounds. Steph stood up with Wade when he pointed to it down by the trees. She could see it, and then he asked her if she wanted a personal tour. *It might be sentimental to bring up to TJ how you stepped foot in a place so special to him as a child. He doesn't go there anymore, maybe you could bring something back from there, I'm sure he has toys or trinkets still left in there.* Steph giggled at that idea, and she walked with Wade down the path, and then off of it and through the grass.

When they reached the door of the clubhouse, as Wade had called it, Steph suddenly felt uneasy. Her queasiness in the morning was sometimes overpowering, but this was more. She was tense about giving in to Wade's quest without TJ knowing where she was. She reached into the pocket of her baggy heather gray sweatpants to retrieve her phone, and that's when Wade abruptly snatched it from her. "It's a surprise, remember?" When he put her cell phone into the back pocket of his jeans, Steph knew coming there was a mistake. She tried to back away, but Wade already had turned the doorknob, took ahold of her arm, and forced her inside.

Steph heard herself demand, *let go of me,* and then she recognized how the two of them were not alone. There was a man, dressed in charcoal gray hospital scrubs. He had short gray hair and wire rim glasses. There was what looked like a hospital stretcher, covered in solid white sheets. She saw some instruments on a square metal tray, which looked like surgical tools. Before she could escape, she was overpowered. Her screams went unheard, deep in the backyard of the Morgan's mansion. She was tied down. Her sweatpants and underwear were removed. Her legs were put in stirrups. She fought until she became groggy from the general anesthetic, which the man in scrubs administered to her through a forced needle in the bend of her arm. When Steph closed her eyes, Wade left the clubhouse.

The doctor opened her cervix and then reached for one of the instruments on the tray beside the stretcher. He began to scrape the lining of Steph's uterus to dislodge the placenta. The fetus, he was told, was eleven weeks old. The fetus was Steph's baby, a baby she and TJ wanted to bring into this world. No matter the timing in their young lives. No matter how difficult the responsibility became.

The seasoned doctor had done this before. He knew the fetus couldn't come out intact. He hadn't dilated Steph's cervix efficiently for that. The tiny parts were soft enough to break apart as he removed them, one by one. He typically would use an ultrasound scan to guide him through this gruesome process. Here, he was just working with what he had.

It was all over in twelve minutes. And just as quickly afterward, there was no trace of anything that occurred in that clubhouse. Steph opened her eyes, alone, and found herself lying on uneven wood slabs on the floor inside of the clubhouse. She was weak, and still groggy, and her eyesight was blurred. She started to recall what happened, but her body wasn't yet coherent. She closed her eyes again in that dark clubhouse with the old, half-tattered shades drawn on its two small windows.

MIRROR IMAGE

✳✳✳

TJ had gone looking for Steph outside by the swimming pool and then all over the mansion. He passed through the kitchen three times as Belle and Sonja were still in there talking, and finally eating breakfast. They had known TJ was searching for Steph, and by the third time, Belle spoke.

"You still have not found her?" Belle asked TJ, who looked annoyed. "No, and she's not answering my texts. I called her, too."

"Did you check the shower?" Sonja suggested.

"Twice!" TJ answered.

"Let's go outside, because she never came in through here," Belle said, standing up from the kitchen table and making an attempt to push Sonja's wheelchair.

"There are other entrances," Sonja informed her, "but I agree, let's check the grounds. Maybe she went for a walk?"

There was a ramp, which allowed Belle to safely roll Sonja's chair outside. TJ had gone ahead of them and they all ended up near the swimming pool, at the glass-topped patio table where Steph and TJ had eaten breakfast.

As they stood there, rehashing where Steph might have gone and wondering why she was not answering her phone, Belle spotted something first. Down, a distance away, where the path no longer continued and the trees began, she saw what looked like a person, crawling.

"What is that?" Belle pointed, and then began running, "Oh my God! Steph!" Sonja had no other choice, but to stay stationary as she watched TJ pass up Belle in a run that appeared utterly frantic.

TJ made it to Steph first. He was on the ground with her. She was now curled up into a fetal position, holding her abdomen with her forearm. When Belle reached them, TJ had Steph in his arms. He was sitting on the back of his legs, cradling her, and begging her to tell him what was wrong. Both he and Belle saw the bloodstains on her light heather-gray sweatpants. The crotch area was saturated. "The baby!" Belle exclaimed, fearing and knowing she had lost it. With that much blood, Belle knew Steph was miscarrying.

Steph was crying as TJ rose to his feet with her in his arms. He and Belle made their way with Steph up the hill as she began to lose consciousness again. Belle was out of breath in her long white broomstick skirt, wrinkled and windblown, and she called for an ambulance before they met Sonja on the patio. "Mom, we're losing the baby!" TJ cried out and Sonja looked shocked and pained simultaneously.

"Let's go! Around front! You are going along with us to the hospital!" Belle ordered Sonja, and she objected.

"No, just go, don't wait for me. I'll only slow you down."

"You're coming!" Belle insisted as she took ahold of the handles on the back of the wheelchair and followed TJ in a rush. He led the way around the grounds and within minutes they were meeting the ambulance in the circle drive in front of the mansion.

MIRROR IMAGE

"I don't want to leave her!" TJ cried out to Belle as Steph was loaded up onto a stretcher by two paramedics who guided it into the ambulance.

Belle stood there wanting with every fiber of her being to be with her daughter. But, she told TJ to just go in the ambulance. She would bring his mother with her to the hospital. TJ reached into the front pocket of his jeans and threw a set of keys at her. "Take the van that's in the detached four-car garage! It's equipped for my mom."

It was additional work, but Belle managed to get Sonja into the van and then back out again after they arrived at the hospital. The two of them thought they would find TJ in the waiting room of the emergency room, but they didn't. It wasn't busy or overly crowded, as Belle found a corner chair and she sat beside Sonja in the wheelchair. They had spoken very little on the drive, other than Sonja directing Belle where to turn and when.

"What was Steph doing way down there, on your grounds?" Belle asked, wondering if that hike had caused her to overexert and miscarry the baby.

"I don't know. We do have a clubhouse behind the trees, but it's been unused for years and she should not have gone trekking through the land and brush alone." Sonja felt equally as confused and sad as Belle.

"I wish we would hear something," Belle sighed.

"Thank you," Sonja began. "You're her mother, I know you should have been in that ambulance with her. Instead, you saw to it that the invalid got loaded up to tag along."

"Stop right there," Belle told her, knowing it was TJ's place to be with Steph because it was his baby, too. "You are a person, not an invalid. You would have been just as special to this baby as any of us," Belle choked on her tears. She was already speaking as if the baby was lost.

"I'll never forget what you've done for me. No matter what the outcome today," Sonja told her. "I adore you."

From where she was seated, Belle leaned in to Sonja and the two women met in an embrace which felt like home. They both were crying for their loss, a loss they knew would be confirmed shortly. And then TJ walked into the waiting room, his face wet with tears.

Chapter 16

The lights were dim in the hospital room they entered as TJ held the door for Belle while she pushed Sonja's wheelchair inside. Neither one of them had asked if Steph lost the baby. Tears continued to roll off of TJ's cheeks as they walked and Sonja had reached for his hand and held it.

Steph was lying in the only occupied bed and Belle moved quickly to her once she settled Sonja near the bedside. Belle leaned over her daughter and put both of her hands on her face. Steph's eyes were open and extremely teary. "Oh honey, I'm so sorry," Belle spoke softly, already knowing. No one had to say the words.

Sonja looked at TJ and whispered, "What happened? What caused it?" That's when Steph abruptly pulled away from her mother and spoke, angrily.

"You mean *who!*" Steph's words confused both Belle and Sonja as TJ shook his head.

"We don't know for sure, Steph. Your memory, it's foggy. We can't accuse him!" TJ was near tears again and Belle asked to know what was going on. She wanted answers from her daughter. Now.

"I remember enough to know that your father did this to me! He took our baby away from us!" Steph was yelling in that small hospital room when the doctor entered.

"Something definitely happened," the middle-aged doctor in a white lab coat with a skinhead of brown hair, spoke in a matter-of-fact yet gentle tone. "After examining your daughter, I know an abortion was performed today. She did not miscarry. The bleeding you saw when you found her was the aftermath of a rushed surgical procedure."

"Oh dear God!" Sonja exclaimed, fearing Wade was responsible. She suddenly felt sick to her stomach, not wanting to believe he was capable of such a horrific act.

MIRROR IMAGE

"Start from the beginning!" Belle demanded, feeling the same anger surface as she had felt the night Gabi was taken from her.

Steph explained that somehow she and Wade ended up walking to the clubhouse, but she couldn't remember why. She recalled what looked like a stretcher, some surgical instruments, and a strange man wearing hospital scrubs. She didn't remember both of the men pinning her down, tying her up, stripping her from the waist down, and forcing her feet into stirrups. She only remembered her fear of Wade at the front door of the clubhouse, being forced inside by his hand gripping her arm too tightly, and then seeing the surroundings. She remembered the terror of something terrible about to happen and she was trembling now as she told her mother and TJ's mother what she knew for certain. TJ did not want to believe her, and still didn't as he heard Steph's story again. "This wasn't a miscarriage, you heard the doctor!" Steph raised her voice and directed those words at TJ.

"The police have been called as I'm certain a crime was committed today, that is if the abortion was not consensual," the doctor was careful with his word choice, but still he angered Steph.

"I wanted my baby!" her tone escalated to a scream and then she immediately burst into tears. Belle held her close as TJ walked over to the window and stood there, staring out of it. Sonja rolled her wheelchair over to her son, and spoke. "You cannot protect your father, and I cannot protect you anymore. He has to pay."

"If he did this, if he is responsible for ending my baby's life, I will kill him with my bare hands," TJ's response startled Sonja. She looked down at her lap, and never said a word. What she was thinking, however, was she needed to retract her words. She could still protect her son. And she would. He had his entire life ahead of him. She, on the other hand, really didn't have much to live for. *If she got caught.*

※※※

Steph was inconsolable, so instead of releasing her from the hospital to go home to rest, the doctor ordered a sedative to relax her for a few hours. TJ sat in silence by her bedside. The police had already been there to receive Steph's statement. Now, two detectives were entering Morgan Fashion, Inc. to question Wade. He was sly and slick and always remained one step ahead of the detectives, so they expected to once again come up empty-handed with any evidence to allow the alleged charges to stick. A few more detectives had already made their way to the clubhouse on the Morgan estate. If something shady had happened there, they were counting on even the smallest shred of proof.

"I need some air," Belle spoke, and then looked at Sonja. "Join me?" Sonja nodded her head, and Belle pushed her out of the hospital room after TJ again made a gentleman's effort to hold the door.

The afternoon sun was shining and it was a pleasant eighty degrees outside. Belle just kept walking through the hospital grounds and then they ended up on a sidewalk that led them to a nearby park. There was a gazebo as well as a pavilion overlooking a nearby pond. Belle rolled Sonja's wheelchair underneath a shade tree, just slightly off the paved path, and near the gazebo.

"I'm sorry, I should have asked if you needed some water or something before we came so far out here," Belle said, as she sat down on the ground beside Sonja's wheelchair. She was still wearing her long, white skirt but at this point she didn't care if it was grass stained.

"I'm fine. What I need is to talk about this and you are the only one I want to confide in," Sonja spoke, sadly. "I cannot believe this happened today. It's horrific. I don't know how our children, especially Steph, will recover from this."

"I'm so angry," Belle interjected. "I'm reverting back to how I felt when Gabi died so suddenly and freakishly. I don't know how much more of this I can take, and it's all at the hands of *him*."

"He will pay," Sonja spoke with her voice low as there were more people out and about, enjoying the beautiful spring weather at the park. The paved path, which Belle had been pushing Sonja on, was especially active.

"But what if, once again, the police have no proof?" Belle asked, believing that could happen. "He seems to be skilled at slipping through the cracks."

"I'm certain the police will come up empty-handed," Sonja spoke, feeling disgusted. "And I think we should play along…"

"Excuse me?" Belle asked.

"I watched TJ in the hospital room, he doesn't want to believe his father is capable. He's fighting what he already knows is the truth because he loves Wade. I think you and I should take Wade's side." Belle's eyes widened and her brow creased as she continued to listen to Sonja. "We should pretend to believe that Steph had a miscarriage and the trauma from it could be causing her to fabricate a story. Her thought process is unclear. Wade originally suggested she abort the baby, and maybe that's manifested in her mind and she actually believes it happened?"

"Just how long do we keep up that crazy charade? And why?" Belle asked, knowing Sonja was up to something.

"I'll need your help, obviously," Sonja said, referring to herself being confined to a wheelchair. "I want it to be quick, I don't want him to have a chance to talk his way out of anything. I don't want him to suffer, but I do prefer that he knows it's over for him before he actually takes his last breath."

"Are you kidding me?" Belle spoke in disbelief, and then looked around, suddenly feeling immoral, as if she and Sonja could be overheard and caught.

"Don't tell me you have not thought about it? Think of your sister, and now our grandbaby..." The look in Sonja's eyes was almost frightening, but Belle could relate. She had never ceased thinking about her sister. And the idea of seeking revenge still haunted her thoughts. She, afterall, did have a loaded handgun inside of her suitcase at the Morgan estate.

"There's a part of me that wants to leave you, right here, sitting under this tree, and run, just run, from you, this city, and everything that has gone wrong at the hands of Wade Morgan," Belle expressed exactly how she felt, and Sonja grinned when she heard her add, "But, since when has running away ever solved anything?"

One year later

Chapter 17

Belle stood in front of the full-length mirror in her bedroom on the third floor of the townhouse in Brunswick. *A lot can happen in a year* seemed to Belle like the mother of all understatements.

Steph was sitting in a desk near the back of a classroom, completing a final exam for an elective course she knew for certain she would never need. She forced herself to concentrate. She had worked tirelessly to bring all of her college scores back up at the University of Maine, and failing one final would defeat her efforts.

Sonja sat on the cream-colored leather seat inside the black stretch limousine as it drove up to the curb, downtown Silver Spring. She looked up, through the window, to see the brand new sign just erected a few days ago on her building in the business hub of the city. *Safe & Sound,* it read, and underneath the bold letters were the italicized words, *mental and emotional healing.* Repeated, on the building's glass door entrance, were those same words in conjunction with her name. *Sonja Morgan, Licensed Clinical Social Worker.* She waited for her trusted chauffeur, a burly black man named Mario, with an afro as big as his heart, to retrieve her wheelchair before he opened her door, lifted her out of the limo and into her *chair on wheels* as he liked to refer to it. It was time to get to work. Finally, Sonja was able to begin helping others again because she had discovered how to heal herself first.

In the mirror, Belle could see her king-sized bed in the background. It was still unmade. She used to enjoy folding back and slipping in between the cool sheets at nighttime. She had always thought of it as a little piece of heaven to lie down and close her eyes after a productive day. That feeling though wasn't from the comfort of the expensive mattress or the freshly washed sheets, as she had always believed. Just a few months ago, Belle realized exactly what had given her that peaceful feeling at the end of every day. It was lying next to a man she

MIRROR IMAGE

had committed to and with him she had built a family and a good life. Belle had not had a sound night's sleep since she recognized the reality of that. She missed her husband lying next to her. She missed things about him that she never seemed to be conscious of before now. Some of those things were important, some trivial. Clint's side of the bed was undisturbed, unwrinkled. And the pillow still had its full, fluffy shape at the dawn of every new day.

The two of them had been separated for almost three months. It was Clint who walked out. He said *she had changed*. He said he *could not understand who she was anymore*. He came to visit the kids a few nights per week, and every weekend. Sometimes, Belle would leave so they could have the house and share the fun things they used to do together in the yard or somewhere else special. Other times, Clint would take both Skylar and Sammy with him. He was renting a brand new apartment, downtown, not too far from the bank. They always traded a few words and looks, but it was never enough. It was about their children now. Not about them.

Belle turned and stood near the foot-end of the bed. She lifted up one knee and rested it on the patterned cushion of the cedar chest. The pant legs of her faded flared denim were long and rested over top of her bare feet, with toenails painted sky blue. Her white lycra v-neck shirt was sleeveless and borderline boxy. Belle had this conversation with herself almost every morning. *I could stop drinking. I could be compliant again instead of voicing my opinions and standing my ground. But, that wouldn't be me. Too much happened and, yes, I have changed.* The mirror's image was still the same, but the woman was not.

"Mom!" Skylar interrupted her thoughts as she turned around, put both of her feet on the carpet again, and listened to her fifteen-year-old daughter. "You and I are both going to be late for the last day of school if we don't get going! Sammy's already in the car." Belle smiled, and reached for her long-sleeved peach Oxford shirt lying on the bed. She slipped it on, left it unbuttoned, and rolled up each sleeve twice while she stepped into her dark brown wedges on the floor. One last look in her full-length mirror. "I'm ready, kiddo. Let's go."

Belle's children were doing okay. Just okay. Not great. Not wonderful. And not the happiest she had ever seen them when their family all lived under the same roof. But, Belle reminded herself how that's life. Families break up. Sometimes things change. And learning to be okay is a choice. She only hoped her children would learn from her quiet grace. She was hurting, knowing her marriage had crumbled, but she held her head high and remained positive. She had not accepted defeat, but she had not fought either.

Steph, for several months, continued to reel from the traumatic experience of being forced to abort her baby. One year later, now, she was finally focused on college again. She had decided to study to become a gynecologist. The irony of what had happened to her and the need to understand it, led her to want to help other women as a career. She believed if she put her whole heart into her quest to become a doctor, she wouldn't have to focus on how broken it was. She and TJ parted ways one year ago. It was a joint decision between their mothers, and inevitably the two of them, after all of their lives drastically changed one crazed night in Silver Spring.

MIRROR IMAGE

Belle had followed Sonja's lead. It was a crazy plan, but after what had happened to Steph in that clubhouse at the hands of Wade, Belle felt rage. A rage that had sparked and slowly began to burn when Gabi died. Then, it ignited into a full blown inferno when Steph became a victim. Sonja was right, Wade needed to be stopped.

***

Lure him to the clubhouse. That was the plan one year ago. TJ had just brought Steph home from the hospital. She was tucked into bed in his room. He had heard his father come home. It had been a stressful, tiring day at Morgan Fashion, Inc. for Wade as he had spent too much of his day answering questions from the police. There was no warrant for his arrest as there wasn't a shred of proof to support Steph's accusations. Wade was compliant with the detectives, but he had been so anxious knowing the police were in his building and just one floor up drug dealings were taking place. He had expected the security guard in the lobby to have followed protocol and alerted for all activity to cease until law enforcement left the building. And, in addition, he had to convince the police that he was present in board meetings all morning, and had not been on the grounds of his estate.

All Wade wanted to do was rush en route to his bedroom, consume his evening heroin fix, and sleep. But, TJ met him at the base of the stairway in the living room, just as he had entered the front door and closed it.

"Thomas Jude," Wade spoke, feigning to appear sympathetic to what his son and girlfriend had gone through today.

"You never answered my calls today," TJ told him.

"I had board meetings all morning and then this afternoon I had the pleasure of dealing with police detectives." Wade was conscious of the fact that he could in no way, shape or form, mock or criticize Steph to TJ.

"Steph swears it was you," TJ spoke, not wanting to believe it, but having his doubts in spite of the fact that he had been arguing with Steph all day in his father's defense. He just didn't want to believe it. His father could not be responsible for *killing* his baby. "Do you have a solid alibi?"

"My board members can vouch for me," Wade said, with confidence and ease.

"That's not what I asked!" TJ raised his voice. "I know damn well your people would back you up, sacrificing their own lives." TJ had never came right out and told his father that he knew about the drugs, both his addiction and dealings. But, there had been times, in anger or frustration, and now doubt, when he implied he knew.

"I was at the office, Teej," Wade spoke softly and TJ almost flinched. He could still be the father he loved with all of his heart. "I have not been to your clubhouse in years. I did not hire anyone to hurt your girlfriend and, God forbid, *take* your baby."

"Well, someone did," TJ responded, fighting back the tears which wanted to spring into his eyes. "Someone is responsible for Steph's pain. My pain. I don't see us making it through this if you murdered our baby. You're my father for God's sake!" The tears were present in TJ's eyes now, and Wade took advantage of his vulnerability.

He walked over to his son and reached for him. He took both of his hands and placed them on top of TJ's shoulders. He squeezed affectionately, but firmly. "Yes, I am. And, despite what I said about the premature timing and a baby ruining your future when you first shocked me with the news, I wanted you to experience what it feels like to be *a father*. You've brought me great joy, son." That conversation was over. TJ took a step closer and fell into his father's arms and there wasn't room in his heart for any more accusations. He didn't want to believe it, so he now chose not to. Siding with his father, he knew, would cost him the love of his life.

Underneath the bottom banister rung on the stairway, above the last step where TJ was standing, was a professional grade listening device called a bug. Sonja had planted it there, expecting TJ to confront his father the moment he stepped foot inside the front door. TJ had no idea that upstairs in Sonja's bedroom, she and Belle had been listening to the whole conversation between father and son. TJ had fallen for Wade's lies. He had chosen to take sides with a man he knew he shouldn't completely trust.

Belle had been sitting on the end of Sonja's queen-sized bed on top of the pale pink duvet, where she had parked close in her wheelchair close. They both listened and shook their heads when the conversation they had been eavesdropping on was over.

"He's a very convincing man, especially if you love him," Sonja spoke first.

"So I've gathered," Belle said, thinking of Gabi. "I, however, do not love him nor have I ever, so I feel like I have an advantage here over both your son and you."

"So you will help me?" Sonja asked Belle, and she fell silent.

When Belle finally spoke, she told Sonja exactly what she was thinking. "I am a mother of three children, a wife to the same man for twenty years, a respected guidance counselor at school and in the community. Can I really take someone's life and still expect all of that, all of who I am, to remain unchanged? I've asked myself that question over and over again since the night I found my sister dead on her living room floor. Sounds brutal, and it was. Can something like that change you?" Belle asked aloud, and then answered her own question, "Yes, most definitely." Sonja continued to listen to Belle speak. "I want to take my daughter and get the hell out of here. I never want to see him again. I'm afraid of what could happen if I do. I know he's in this house now and I believe he's responsible for my daughter's loss today."

"He is," Sonja spoke, her face expressionless. "And, trust me, he will get away with that, too."

"Why do you hate him so much?" Belle asked.

Sonja turned her wheelchair away for a moment and rolled it back and forth near the foot end of the bed where Belle was still seated. Belle noticed again how the strength in Sonja's arms was all she had to work with in order to move, and she made it look effortless. "Husbands and wives are supposed to feel like they would do anything for each other. Take a bullet. A knife. Name your poison. I used to feel that way about Wade. He was my world, along with our son," Sonja paused before continuing. "And, as it turned out, I wasn't the only one who believed she couldn't live without my husband. As happy and in love with each other as we were, that wasn't enough for him. I wasn't enough. I had no idea, absolutely no idea. If I had, maybe I wouldn't-. No, not maybe," Sonja corrected herself and the look in her eyes was pure hatred. "I would not be in this chair." Belle furrowed her brow, but before she could say she didn't understand, Sonja finished speaking. "She was crazy in love with him, *crazy* being the operative word. She was behind the wheel of the truck that veered off the road and onto the sidewalk, and crashed into me. She was probably disappointed that the accident didn't take my life. But, really it did."

By now, Belle had her hand over her mouth in disbelief. "My God, indirectly what happened to you *was* Wade's fault!"

"How polite of you to say *indirectly*," Sonja spoke sarcastically. "I'm sure you may have used that word to describe Wade's part in your sister's death as well. Well, what it comes down to is he is a monster."

"And he must be stopped," Belle added.

"Yes, but do either one of us have what it takes?" Sonja asked, realizing the truth in what Belle had said. Rage had made them both want to end Wade's life, but they weren't like him. They both had a conscience. *Didn't they?*

TJ had made his way to his mother's room. She was the one he turned to whenever he had mixed emotions about his father. When he approached her bedroom door to knock, he had heard voices. He recognized Belle's voice and his mother's. He was going to leave and return later, but then he listened to their conversation. He knew they both believed Wade was guilty. He still didn't. Even with Steph's accusations, TJ remained sided with his father. It was the mention of his mother's accident that had sent him reeling. He stood by the door, knees buckling, when he learned the truth. *His mother's accident, when he was just a boy, was intentional. His father was having an affair. His father's then mistress was to blame for his mother's pain and the loss of her legs. The loss of the vibrant person she once was.*

At that moment, the difference between TJ and his mother was, when he felt rage, he didn't think about it. He acted.

Chapter 18

TJ pounded his fist three times on his father's bedroom door. This was an incredibly spacious mansion of just under eleven thousand square footage. They all sometimes retreated to their separate bedrooms which were sizeable enough to feel comparable to a living room or family room of any home. They weren't much of a family anymore, and hadn't been for a very long time. But, just in the past two days, having Belle and Steph there, it had begun to feel like a home again. TJ wanted them to be a part of all of their lives. The two them already had a way of bringing them together. Sonja was a different person, or so much like herself again when Belle was around. A baby had brought them together, and he now believed his father tore that apart just like he ruined their family ten years ago. If there was one thing TJ had always hung onto was he believed his father loved his mother and would have done anything for her. He felt utterly disgusted as he pounded on the door for the final time. *His father's mistress had rundown his mother.*

The door was locked and TJ took one step back, raised his right foot in the air as high as he could manage, and kicked in the door with the charcoal gray Brooks tennis shoe he was wearing. The bedroom was empty, but he could hear the shower water running in the bathroom. On a high-legged, rectangular-shaped table pushed up against the far wall near the bathroom was a small baggie of a white powdery substance. There was a compact mirror placed beside it. TJ had never looked for it in his father's possession before. He knew he was an addict and a dealer, but he had chosen to separate himself from that side of Wade Morgan. Part of him was afraid of what his reaction would be if he had confronted his father. *Would he deny it? Threaten him? Or would he convince him to cross over to that lifestyle?*

TJ heard the shower water shut off, so he backed up from the drug table and walked over to the window that spanned nearly the entire wall. He stood there, looking down at the view of the swimming pool, and their pond on the far side of the property. Even farther, he could see the rooftop of the clubhouse. A place where he would go to feel safe. A place where his baby's life was taken today because his father wanted control. Wade Morgan's days of being in command of his son's life were now over.

Wade opened the door, wearing a long, bulky burgundy towel wrapped low around his waist. His blond hair was wet and disheveled from just having been towel dried. He saw his son immediately as TJ turned around from facing the window. He noticed the locked door to his bedroom had been kicked in, and part of the door frame was now a section of splintered wood.

MIRROR IMAGE

"What is going on?" Wade asked in a demanding tone. He locked the door for a reason. His drug paraphernalia was unhidden, and visible right there on the table.

"You tell me, dad. What is going on? No, wait, you will just feed me more lies!" TJ raised his voice and Wade walked over to him. His bare feet were still wet from the shower and he was leaving water droplets on the dark hardwood flooring in his bedroom.

"I thought we were clear. I told you, Steph is just lashing out at me. She needs to direct her pain and anger at someone because she had a miscarriage and she's hurting. I was the one who suggested she abort the baby and that's coming back on me now. It's okay, I-"

"Stop!" TJ screamed at him. "Stop doing what you do so well. Stop lying to me."

Usually, not a voice carried or a sound was heard coming from the many rooms in that house. Everyone was always in their separate corners and wanted to be left alone. Right now, however, Sonja was in her wheelchair at the end of the same corridor that she had just heard her son's voice coming from.

"Lying to you about what?" Wade asked, standing directly in front of his son. Even in his bare feet, Wade was still an inch taller than TJ. They were both over six feet tall with broad shoulders and fit torsos. TJ's dark hair contrasted Wade's blond. As did TJ's brown eyes and Wade's blue eyes. Their voices sounded similar. Their walk was the same. All the rest, TJ knew he inherited from his mother. He wanted to be good like his mother, but right now he was fighting so much pain and disappointment.

"Who was driving the truck that hit my mother?"

"Thomas Jude that was a decade ago and we've been over this. It was an accident. Charges were never filed." Wade was taken aback to have this subject brought up again.

"You told me it was a man who was behind the wheel…" TJ spoke. "You never wanted to talk in detail about it. I thought that was because you were hurting so badly, but there was more to it, right dad?"

"Son, I–" Before Wade could say anymore, TJ wrapped both of his hands around his father's neck.

"Your mistress, a woman you were fucking while you claimed to love my mother, ran her down!" TJ's eyes were piercing and only inches away from his father's, and Wade was struggling for air. He took both of his hands and attempted to push off of his son's chest and force him away from him. TJ only tightened his hands around his father's throat. "Admit it, you son of a bitch!" TJ screamed and Wade instantly tried to grab at his son's throat, face, hair, anything he could take ahold of to force him to release the death grip he had on his throat. TJ reacted by throwing him down onto the floor, straddling his chest and resealing his grip on his throat.

Wade was struggling to speak, but he knew he had better oblige. "Okay, okay. It…is…true. I didn't know…she…was crazy. I never wanted your…mother…hurt."

"She was more than just *hurt!* You know she lost her will to live! You took that away from her!" TJ beat Wade's head against the flooring and Wade begged him to stop. "And my baby! Tell me what you did to Steph today in that clubhouse!"

TJ was adamant and he had a crazed look in his eyes that Wade had never seen before. If he didn't fight back, his son would kill him. Wade's adrenaline kicked in and he gathered enough strength to start fighting back. He struggled and then finally managed to force TJ off of his chest to release his grip around his throat. Arms were flailing, legs were kicking. There were fist punches. Wade's eye was bleeding, TJ's nose felt broken. They were both back on their feet. Wade stood there completely naked as his towel was lost in all of the crazy movements. TJ stood just a few feet away and he backed up a few more steps. "I don't know you. A man who hides behind his fortune, his power, his drugs, and a guilty conscience. I can't handle what you did to my baby."

Their faces and hands were bloody. Wade managed to grab the towel he had lost and wrap it around his waist again. He didn't really care, as only his son was in the room. He never saw Sonja through the broken door frame, sitting in her wheelchair across the hallway. She had heard their fight, the words they had exchanged, and now she was watching them both and witnessing as their relationship unraveled.

"You will understand one day," Wade spoke in no uncertain terms. "You are embarking on the prime of your life. You have dreams to fulfill."

"I would throw all of that away in a heartbeat to have a family with Steph, to have her by my side. That," TJ raised his voice, "is the difference between you and me!"

"Love doesn't last," Wade spoke adamantly. "Money and power and a little help to keep yourself above the clouds," Wade said, referring to the heroin, "are all you need. And I think it's time you loosen up with me." Wade walked over to the table against the wall and retrieved one of the small baggies with the white powdery substance inside. "Try it. Let your father introduce you to something amazing. Your tension is eating you alive, my boy. You may think you hate me now, but this will put all of that shit out of your head. Join me…" TJ was silent. He didn't know if he was contemplating actually giving in to his father, or if he was in shock. He had heard the rumors, his mother told him the truth. His father was a druggie. An addict. A dealer. TJ just never sought the proof. He never wanted to see this for himself.

He watched his father walk over to the bed and he reached underneath one of his pillows. He was taken aback when he saw him holding a pistol. And then Wade pointed it at him. "On your knees," Wade ordered him.

"What? Dad? No! You're not going to force me to snort that shit!" TJ was suddenly scared out of his mind. Wade placed the baggie on top of the cherry red duvet at the foot-end of his bed. He dumped it directly onto the bedding. He pointed the gun at TJ. "On your knees, Thomas Jude. Close one nostril with your finger and inhale with the other." Wade pulled back the pistol's slide.

"You are going to have to shoot me first. I am not like you, nor do I ever want to be." TJ spoke with his voice calm and Wade grabbed him by the back of his dark hair. He started to force him to his knees and that's when Sonja came barreling through the door in her wheelchair. Both men turned to find her. Neither TJ nor Wade knew she was there until she was in the room with them, and holding a pistol of her own.

"Mom! No. You need to leave. Now!" TJ was scared for himself, but more scared for his mother now. She was helpless and he knew Wade could overpower her in an instant.

"I can handle your father," Sonja spoke, directing her handgun at him.

"You could never swat at a fly, or flatten a spider with your shoe. You expect me to believe you are capable of putting a bullet in me? I don't think so. You better go, unless you want to watch the show. Your son is about to become a man." Wade held his gun against TJ's temple on the side of his head, and he attempted to force him again to his knees. TJ was at a loss. If he fought his father, he could be shot, or his mother could be. He started to bend his knees toward the floor, near the foot-end of the bed.

"Wade. Look at me," Sonja spoke. "I want you to know that this is it. I want to see your face, those bloodshot eyes, when I tell you I don't want you to suffer. I know what suffering is. I do, however, want you to die."

Three shots were fired. And each one of those bullets went into Wade's heart.

Chapter 19

"We could tell the police exactly what I came upon in here. Your father was forcing you to use." Sonja sat in her wheelchair with her back turned to the body of her husband. TJ was squatted down in front of her, holding both of her hands, which were trembling from what she had just done.

TJ had cried when he checked his father's pulse but found none, and then frantically rushed over to his mother. "I don't know, I can't think clearly!" TJ snapped just as he saw Belle and Steph, moving too quickly for her condition, making their way through the broken doorway.

"What happened?" Belle demanded to know as Steph grabbed ahold of her tightly when she spotted Wade's bloody body on the floor. Belle felt incredible panic and looked directly at Sonja as her thoughts raced. *She and Sonja had come to an understanding. Killing him would not be worth the consequences.*

TJ had placed the gun Sonja used on the floor by the front wheel of her chair. "My mother saved me from being forced to use my father's drug of choice."

"Oh my God!" Steph said, letting go of her mother and running into TJ's arms. He held her and she cried. Belle took a few more steps inside of that bedroom and knelt down in front of Sonja. She held her tightly. "You are going to be okay. You saved your son. Remember that!" Belle completely understood now. *A mother would kill to save her child.*

"That is what we will tell the police!" Steph blurted out. "It's the truth! *He* was a monster." Steph glared at TJ's father's body, recalling and knowing she would never forget what he had forced her to go through.

"I think we should handle this," TJ spoke to the three women alone in that room with him. "Belle, I need you to grab two or three suitcases out of the closet in here and pack up all that he owned. Make it look like he was going away. Steph, get rid of the drugs. Flush them. Mom, you have a spare chair, right? I need to wheel the body out of here." The three women stared at him in disbelief. *Could this really work? Or were they all going to go down as accomplices?*

"I won't lose my mother!" TJ said, looking at Steph and then at Belle. And they understood. Her life had already been stolen from her when she lost the use of her legs. It was time for Sonja to be free of Wade, and start anew.

TJ wrapped up his father's body in a spare duvet that he found in the linen closet out in the hallway. In an extra wheelchair, he folded Wade's covered body into a sitting position and then strapped it in. TJ instructed his mother and Steph to stay behind. Steph was too weak, and his mother would have to be carefully pushed through the dark in her wheelchair to get there. There were no free hands to get her down there.

Belle followed TJ on the wheelchair path, leading to the patio near the swimming pool. In each hand, she was carrying two large suitcases, packed full. It was dark out there, as they purposely turned on no outside lights. Even though the help went home for the night, TJ didn't want to take any chances. They made their way further downhill and then off the beaten path toward the clubhouse. There was a light bulb hanging above the door and TJ pulled the chain from it when he walked in first, pushing the body on wheels. Belle took one step inside that clubhouse and shuddered. That was where her daughter had gone through trauma and her grandbaby's life was taken. She still had not changed out of her long, white broomstick skirt. She looked down as she set both of the suitcases onto the uneven floorboards at her feet inside of the clubhouse. That floor was so filthy she could no longer see the white of her Tom's shoes. At that moment she could not believe her daughter didn't end up with a serious infection in that unsterile environment when her body was helpless at the hands of a doctor whom Wade had paid off.

"So you're just leaving the body in here? TJ, the police were just here today and you know they could be back tomorrow!" Belle was afraid TJ's plan was far from foolproof when his only answer was to leave a body and suitcases packed full of clothes and belongings inside of a building which was under police investigation.

"I know what I'm doing," TJ told her as he left the body in the wheelchair, and walked clear across the room. Belle watched him reach into his pocket for a single silver key, and then he bent down in front of a wall vent. The vent was dirty and dusty and TJ moved his fingers back and forth over an indent in the top right corner of it. He then forced the key inside and turned it. And when he did, the wall gave away. The entire wall shifted underneath the palms of both of TJ's hands. He slid it back with ease like a sliding door. He pulled another chain beneath a light bulb and he stared at the secret room. He turned to find Belle taking one, two, three, fast steps toward him. "Oh dear God!" she exclaimed.

"I guess there was no time for the good doctor to move his things out," TJ said, also looking at a stretcher with white sheets, and a metal tray with surgical tools placed on it. The sight repulsed him. Just on the other side of the wall, the police had searched the clubhouse. Now, this side of the wall would also hide his father's body. *Every boy should have a secret room*, TJ remembered his father telling him. It was fascinating then for an eight-year-old. The admiration TJ had for his father all of his life had instantly died with him.

Belle stood near TJ, also experiencing a roller coaster of emotions herself. The man, who was responsible for killing both her sister and a baby whom she would have called her first grandchild, was dead. And she didn't feel any better. There was no difference. Dead or alive, Wade Morgan had still caused her pain, and his life ending tonight had not changed anything for her.

✳ ✳ ✳

What was meant to be just a few days spent in Silver Spring was exactly that. Belle and Steph left the Morgan estate early the following morning. All night long the four of them had been awake and talking, and arguing at times. Steph had initially vowed to stand by TJ's side as he dealt with what happened. The four of them agreed to take this secret to their graves. *Tell no one. Just move on with your lives.* Through the tears of their own goodbye, which literally took hours to talk through, Belle and Sonja agreed it would be best to cease all contact between each other and their children. At least, for awhile. They couldn't force their children to say goodbye and break their ties, but they did strongly suggest giving *it one year. Walk away from this craziness. Put it behind you. Start anew. If you're meant to find your way back to each other, you will.* Their mothers agreed, but it was a ludicrous idea that both Steph and TJ initially firmly rejected.

Then, Sonja had privately convinced TJ to let Steph go in order to protect her. *Did he really want the police to interrogate her? She had been through enough. She may not be able to handle knowing your father was killed and his body was hidden. In time, she could turn on us. We don't know for sure. We could both end up in prison.*

TJ ended up siding with his mother. What she had done for him was risky and selfless. She saved him. And now he would stand by her, and protect her. Above anyone else.

Belle, in turn, tried her damndest to convince her daughter to find a safe haven. *TJ and his mother needed to deal with what had happened, and she needed to grant them the time and space to do so. Steph also needed to put herself first. She had a traumatic ordeal to heal from.* Parting ways seemed like the sensible answer, but it hurt like hell for all of them.

Chapter 20

So it had been one year. Belle sat behind her desk in the guidance counselor quarters of the junior high school. There wasn't much on her schedule today, unless one of the students wanted to pop in her office on the last day of school. She was thinking and wondering what Steph and TJ would do now. She knew her daughter. She was pining away for that young man. She also knew so much had changed in TJ's life, and Belle reminded Steph of that when they spoke on the phone recently. *You need to consider just letting him go.* What Belle didn't know was that her daughter had struggled with *letting go* and still had not been able to release TJ from her mind, nor her heart.

MIRROR IMAGE

The day after his father died, TJ dressed in a designer black suit with polished black dress shoes, a white pressed shirt and a power red tie. He was a complete mess on the inside, but looked flawlessly composed on the exterior. He walked into his father's office building, on a mission to purify Morgan Fashion, Inc. He called an emergency meeting. His father's secretary followed his wishes and gathered all four hundred and nineteen employees into the company's show room. Everyone who had been in the building at that time watched as TJ stepped onto the elevated runway. It was where his father had stood hundreds of times before a show. Before the models, wearing the Morgan label, took the stage for reporters and buyers.

TJ stood in silence and then accepted a cordless microphone, from one of his father's employees, to speak. "Is this everyone?" he asked, checking the volume of his voice projecting in front of him. "Is the third floor currently clear?"

"It's locked sir," a voice told him from the crowd which was made up entirely of his father's staff.

"Very good," TJ replied. He knew it was no secret to anyone present in that building. The third floor was only in operation for one thing. "I'm here to inform you all of a change in our company. This is as much my father's company as it is my mothers, mine, and all of yours. Morgan Fashion Incorporated is your livelihood. I get that." TJ was vastly different from his father. Wade had not once stepped down to the level of his employees. Only the board members had caught glimpses of a human side to Wade Morgan. "My father walked out of his home and this company last night. He's gone indefinitely, and I'm here to take his place." Voices rumbled in the crowd, while some had opted to whisper to those around them. There were a few random claps from the back of the crowded room before it fell completely silent again.

"I will send out a company-wide email to note the changes, but for right now as you all are here and listening to me, I want something done as soon as this meeting adjourns. The third floor. You know who you are. Get rid of it. All of it. This is a fashion house not a drug ward. Not anymore. If you work for this company on the third floor and that is strictly your job, you can leave. If you wish to stay and be productive, talk to me. No one is being kicked out or fired or whatever you all may be thinking right now. I'm just here to redirect all of you to fashion."

As of that day, the day following the evening when his mother shot and killed his father to save him, TJ dropped out of college. He no longer wished to study forestry at the University of Maine. He would be too consumed with running an empire, his father's empire, as the current interim CEO. Sonja had not agreed with his decision, at first, and then TJ promised his mother it would only be temporary. Just until he brought the company back to its roots and had it standing on its own two feet again without the drug dealings. It was something he intended to do to bring respect back to the Morgan name.

TJ had spent the last year working day and night to make that turnaround. He knew being absent from college, at the University of Maine, would also make his promise to stay out of Steph's life easier. *Out of sight, out of mind*, he had hoped, but that never happened. He still thought of her, he still loved her, and he wanted her back more than anything in the world. He also feared she had moved on. *Maybe she believed he and his family were no longer worthy of her?*

MIRROR IMAGE

Belle was unaware of TJ's accomplishments with his father's company. She, like Steph, only knew he quit college. Sonja's recent opening of her new business, *Safe and Sound*, was also something Belle was oblivious of. The one thing Belle knew for certain was she missed that woman. She missed the immediate, almost uncanny, connection they shared and the conversations they had gotten lost in. Calling up Sonja, after one year of no contact to let the dust settle and allow their children to heal and move on, was something Belle was definitely contemplating.

As Belle remained seated behind her desk, lost in thought, the door swung open abruptly without a knock and Jacobi walked in.

"What? Back to your old turf?" Belle asked, standing up to receive a hug from Jacobi's already open arms.

"Oh I wouldn't miss the last day of school, it's a blow-off day, so stop pretending you're hard at work!" Jacobi giggled. She plopped down in the chair in front of Belle's desk and crossed her short legs in yellow stilettos to match her floral yellow sundress. Her skin was already sunkissed in May, and Belle felt a little jealous knowing Jacobi and her husband had just returned from a Caribbean cruise. She didn't want to rush her life into retirement, but she used to wish she and Clint would be able to travel the world together one day when they had an empty nest. Now, her nest was missing her husband.

"So what's changed with you since I've been gone?" Jacobi asked, hoping Belle and Clint had reconciled. She was not Clint's biggest fan, but she did know Belle loved him. She could see the sadness and loneliness in her eyes now.

"Nothing if you're referring to my marriage. We're still separated," Belle answered, looking glum.

"Does he want a divorce?" Jacobi asked.

"We don't speak of it," Belle replied. "In fact, if it doesn't pertain to the kids or ridiculous small talk to fill the air when we do see each other, we don't speak at all."

"Maybe it's time for a date night, time alone to talk, reconnect," Jacobi suggested.

"With my husband who left me?" Belle asked, not feeling optimistic about the idea.

"With your husband who is still your husband," Jacobi told her. "If he really wanted out, if you really wanted out, the two of you would have been divorced by now. It's been months! Work it out already."

***

The problem with attempting to mend her marriage was Belle did not know where to start. She loved Clint. She believed in their relationship, their commitment. But, she failed him in his eyes because she had changed. If he wasn't willing to accept that life and its harsh realities had transformed her, then Belle didn't see the point in making an effort to get her husband back. She needed advice, and some guidance. She needed more than just a push from Jacobi, her greatest cheerleader.

Belle turned to face her laptop computer, already powered on, on top of her desk. She logged onto the Internet and moved her mouse to the Google icon. She placed her fingers on the keyboard and punched in *how to save my marriage.*

It was a broad search, but among self-help books and movie titles with similar wording, Belle's search led her to professional therapists who were available to help, *to rekindle the flame and save marriages. To heal your soul.* She read on.

After clicking and scrolling through a few suggested searches, Belle's eyes moved to a new business called, *Safe and Sound*, where a licensed clinical social worker offered marriage counseling, among other therapies. *Safe and Sound* had a nice ring to it, Belle thought, as she read further and was surprised to find it was located in Silver Spring. One more paragraph down, her eyes widened when she read Sonja Morgan's name.

It had to be an old article. She was no longer practicing. The Internet was like that sometimes. The outdated material was never filtered out. And then Belle found the information about a grand opening and last month's date printed beneath the article. *Sonja was back in business.* Belle beamed at the thought of it. *Sonja deserved to feel happy and whole again.* But, so did Belle. And, she knew just the right person who could help her. Belle bookmarked the webpage for *Safe and Sound*. She would gather the details later. Right now, she needed to log on to Southwest Airlines and book herself a plane ticket to Silver Spring.

✼✼✼

"I need you to watch the kids for a few days. You can stay at the house, Steph will be home from college in two days." Belle had called Clint at the bank and despite him saying he had a minute, he sounded busy.

"Where are you going?" Clint asked, because he felt like he had a right to know. She was still his wife. He did care, and always would.

"To Silver Spring, to see Sonja Morgan," Belle admitted, knowing Clint would fume.

He lowered his voice on the phone. "And you really think that's a good idea?" Belle had not kept the truth from Clint. She told him everything, one year ago, when they returned from Silver Spring. She explained *who* Wade Morgan was and that she made the connection before she and Steph even left town to meet TJ and his parents. She also confided in Clint about what happened that night. Wade Morgan was *shot and killed* by his wife, which resulted in the emergent decision to *hide a dead body*. That was the final straw for Clint. He was a straight shooter and believed his wife was as well. He couldn't understand and he refused to even try. He agreed that Wade Morgan was a monster, because Steph had fallen victim to him, but he could not condone killing him and making it look as if he packed up and skipped town. Forever. While his body rotted just hundreds of feet way on the estate property.

"She's a friend, Clint. I'm just going to reconnect with her." Belle sighed into the phone because she was beginning to believe her decision was incredibly unfair to Steph.

"And what's next? The kids will hook up again and the four of you can sit around and rehash that night?" Clint was being snarky, and Belle took a deep breath.

"Can I tell the kids you'll be staying with them tomorrow night?" Belle asked him.

"Of course," he replied. "I love my children and spending time with them is what I live for."

"Thank you," Belle replied, wondering if he had ever felt that way about her. *Had he lived for their marriage? Their twenty years of love and family?* She had, and she wanted to get that feeling back again. Possibly, with Sonja's help.

✷✷✷

Her flight landed at Ronald Reagan Washington National Airport, which was ten driving miles from Silver Spring. Belle grabbed her overnight bag and hailed a cab. She made it downtown to *Safe and Sound* ten minutes before her appointment time. Belle had called Sonja's secretary two days ago, and requested an appointment to discuss her marriage woes. When she had to give her insurance information, along with her name, she knew didn't want Sonja to know it was her, so she flip flopped Belle Madden quickly in her mind and came up with Madelyn Bell.

Belle sat alone in the waiting room with both her handbag and her overnight traveling bag at her feet. She had worn white linen flared pants, a black light weight scoop neck sweater with three quarter-length sleeves, and black low-heeled sandals on her feet. Her toes and finger nails were painted pale pink and her blonde hair was down in loose curls on her shoulders. She was both excited and nervous to see Sonja today. A part of her wondered if their decision to part ways one year ago was the best one they possibly could have come up with. Belle knew for Steph's sake it probably was. She needed the space to heal, and Belle was incredibly proud of her for deciding to pursue her doctorate in gynecology.

The secretary interrupted Belle's train of thought as she informed her *Ms. Morgan was ready to see her.* Belle was escorted through one door, down a short hallway, and then she stood in front of an open door with a name plate that read, Sonja Morgan, LCSW.

"Ms. Morgan, your client, Madelyn Bell is here to see you." The secretary backed way and Belle stepped through the doorway. Behind her desk, Sonja was seated on a high-back cushioned black chair. "Come in, and please close the door," Sonja spoke in a professional voice, while her face flushed and her eyes widened in astonishment. Belle did as she asked and then walked directly over, behind the desk, to Sonja.

No words were spoken as Belle bent down to Sonja's level and the two of them embraced. Sonja tightened her arms around Belle, and Belle closed her eyes.

"You feel like home," Sonja spoke softly. "All is right with the world when you and I are in the same room together. How is that possible again?"

Belle wholeheartedly agreed, taking Sonja's hands in her own, holding them. "I feel it, too," Belle told her, and they both smiled.

"It's been a year," Sonja said as Belle took a chair from in front of Sonja's desk and carried it around to sit right beside her. "I have to ask. Why did you come here?"

"For more than one reason," Belle spoke, noticing Sonja was wearing a long canary yellow sleeveless linen dress with a white crocheted sweater shell over top. Her wheelchair was nowhere in sight, but Belle had recognized the safety belt on the chair she was seated on behind her desk. "I missed you. I thought it would be safe. And, I need some guidance in my life."

"I missed you as well, so much," Sonja told her. "Yes, it is safe, and I will fill you in on all of that later. First, I want to know how I can help you, as a professional."

"I'm so proud of you for getting this back!" Belle interjected excitedly as she held up and her hands and referred to Sonja's surroundings. Sonja beamed at Belle's words, and waited for her to continue as she watched her expression change to somber. "My husband left me, we've been separated for four months. We are in limbo, and I feel like it is up to me to do something."

"I'm sorry to hear your marriage is in trouble," Sonja spoke sincerely. "I lived in that kind of limbo for far too long. I don't want that for you. Why did he leave?"

"Because I've changed," Belle answered. "He said he doesn't know who I am anymore."

"Do you agree? Have you changed?" Sonja asked her.

"Yes, life has changed me. You know all that has happened to me. Losing my twin sister, for starters, sucked the life out of me."

"But, you've carried on," Sonja pointed out.

"Yes, just not in the way the old Isabelle Madden would have. The Type A personality seems to have taken a hike. I now enjoy drinking, socially and alone, but honestly it's under control. Clint just thinks it's absurd because he abstains from alcohol after a traumatic childhood with an alcoholic father. I've just become more of a free spirit, if you will. I get things done, I take care of my children, but I have such a *fuck it* attitude sometimes."

Sonja giggled under her breath, and Belle waited for her to speak. "It's called loosening up. Middle age," Sonja explained. "I don't know if it's so much that you have changed. Yes, you've suffered tragic loss, but you've grown into your own woman. You were a child in so many ways when you gave birth to your first baby and got married. You strived to do it all and do it right. Look at it as riding a bike. I believe, you just now in your life, have learned to take off the training wheels. Your crutch is no longer needed, or available. Maybe your crutch was in the form of your twin sister? You looked to her for guidance and reassurance. She was the perfect one, you told me. Did you make a decision without her? Did you make a decision without your husband, or have you allowed him to call all the shots because it was just safer that way?"

Belle was listening intently and Sonja continued. "These are things to think about. Long and hard. It may not be all you. I see your husband as not able to handle change, yes, but maybe moreso he's not open to accepting you as your own person. You're his other half."

"And you're very good at this therapist gig," Belle complimented her, and Sonja beamed. "I do hear you, all of your words are ringing true. So, now, what do I do?"

"Belle," Sonja, paused, "you are asking me to make that decision for you. Stop. This is *your* life. Stop turning to others and expecting them to tell you what you should or should not do. You're coming out of that with your husband, obviously, so keep at it, and you will find your true self. And, when that happens, you will know what you want from your marriage and for yourself. This is your life. You only get one. Make wise choices. Or more importantly, make yourself happy."

Chapter 21

Their one-hour session was over before it really began. The two of them had reconnected and felt as if they could talk the hours away, just as they had one year ago when they first met.

"I have two more clients before I can call it a day," Sonja explained. "I hope you are not planning to catch a flight already?"

"Not yet, I can book a hotel room and we can get together later, or tomorrow if you're tired?" Belle didn't want this to be over either.

"Oh here you go again with your hotel nonsense. You tried that once before with me, and remember where that got you?" Sonja smiled and Belle started to shake her head.

"I don't know," Belle almost admitted how she felt skeptical about going back *to that house,* but then she stopped herself.

"I will have my driver bring you to the estate. Make yourself at home, and I will be there in just a couple hours, in time for dinner." Sonja smiled, and Belle who was still seated beside her, reached for her and the two of them were wrapped up in arms again.

"Where's your wheelchair?" Belle asked, as she stood up and returned her chair to its original place.

"For every first session, I put it inside of the closet. I want to make an impression as a therapist first. I don't want any of my clients to see my handicap prior to me being given the chance to help them."

Sonja seemed a little embarrassed, and Belle smiled at her, and replied, "Here you go again with that handicap nonsense!"

✳✳✳

Mario drove Belle in a black stretch limousine to the Morgan estate. Belle had remembered everything about that place. The ritzy exterior and the massive, exquisite interior. She was told that the chef was preparing dinner and the maid had readied her bedroom. The same room she had the last time she stayed there.

Belle put her handbag and her overnight bag inside of the bedroom she was directed to again, and then she went outside. She stood under the pergola on the terrace, where it all began. Her memory flashed back to meeting TJ, meeting Sonja, and feeling incredibly apprehensive about her daughter's future as a young mother. All of it changed overnight in that mansion, and Belle cringed at the thought. She began to walk down the landscape, her black low-heeled sandals clicking on each stepping stone. She passed the swimming pool, stepped into the grass and back onto another path. Before she knew it, she was off that trail and slipping through a row of trees. She was taken aback as soon as she looked up. It was nothing but land, tall green grass, wild flowers, and a few trees just getting their start in the woods. The clubhouse was gone.

When Belle made her way back to the upper level patio terrace, she sat down in a lounge chair and was out of breath. She had thought about the body in that clubhouse and how one day it could be found and the four of them, who were present and aware of what really happened to Wade Morgan that night, could lose their freedom. Obviously, Sonja, or TJ, had ensured that would never happen.

The time passed quickly and soon the French doors leading from the kitchen opened and Sonja rolled herself outside.

"Hi..." Belle said, as it felt wonderful to be with Sonja again.

"Chef told me you declined a drink. Have one with me," Sonja said, pulling out a wine bottle from one side of her wheelchair and two non-stem glasses were tucked in the other. Belle giggled and watched her pop the cork, pour a glass, and hand it over. What a far cry Sonja was from the helpless, full-of-self pity woman Belle had first met.

Belle took a sip and watched Sonja do the same after she had set down the wine bottle on the glass tabletop in front of them. "So what happened to it?" Belle asked, referring to the clubhouse as she looked off in the distance, in that direction.

"It was no longer under investigation. The police seemed to have accepted rather quickly that Wade skipped town. It was blatantly obvious how they welcomed the idea, and appeared to be relieved. The fire was my plan, and TJ handled it. We are so far outside of the city limits. It alarmed no one when we decided to have a slow, controlled burn out here. TJ had two of his firefighter friends on standby. It was an old, unkept building, and we had no use for it anymore."

Belle nodded, but didn't speak for a few minutes as she continued to gaze out at the land. "So you're life, it's good?" Belle asked.

"It's better than it has been in a very long time. Do I think of him? Always. Do I regret what I did? Depends on what kind of mood I'm in," she smirked. "I did what I had to do to save my son."

Belle nodded her head in agreement. "I would do the same for my children. Really, what mother wouldn't act in a moment of danger and desperation?"

"How are your children, especially Steph?" Sonja asked.

"It's taken her a long time to work through her emotions. She's decided to study gynecology. Ironic, isn't it?"

"It's the power of healing," Sonja stated.

"I suppose so," Belle replied. "How about you? What has healed you? You look healthier, you have delved back into your career."

"It was time. Being in this chair is lifelong, but slowly dying inside didn't have to be. I have a son who needs me more than ever because his father is gone. TJ quit school to run Morgan Fashion, and I want him to go back. He said to give him a year, and he would. He's cleaned up the business, if you know what I mean. The millions of dollars in drug dealings no longer are coming in. He is struggling to pay our employees what they've worked for all these years. We're going to sell the estate, there's no need for the two of us to live like royalty. Wade wanted that for us. I discovered, from one of his board members who came to see me, feeling distraught over Wade's disappearance, that Wade started dealing in order to keep the business afloat, pay for my medical bills, and keep this estate."

"Oh my," Belle spoke, sincerely. "That had to be difficult to hear."

"He always vowed to take care of us," Sonja spoke, her face expressionless. "He just never realized all we needed was him. All of him. But, he could never allow himself to be just ours. He desired a mistress. He craved drugs to power through life. There was always something pulling him away from us."

"My problems seem so trivial, compared to yours," Belle said, honestly.

"Never say that," Sonja abruptly replied. "Everyone's pain and struggles are their own. Your marriage is in trouble. That is why you came to see me, isn't it?"

"That, and I missed you. I guess ceasing contact was wise, especially for the kids, but for us maybe not so much." Belle's honesty touched Sonja.

"I've thought about you a million times," Sonja admitted. "I had no idea your marriage was in trouble. You didn't speak much of your husband before."

"I love Clint, but I'm just afraid we've grown too far apart to find our way back," Belle stated, looking down at her wine glass which she was close to emptying.

"So you love him, and I know you love your children," Sonja began. "But, do you love yourself?"

"Excuse me?" Belle asked, feeling embarrassed by the question.

"You heard me," Sonja replied. "When you were nineteen you knew nothing about the world yet, and you had so much growing into your own to do. Have you done that? Have you found yourself?"

"That seems like such a silly question," Belle said, trying to understand it. "I've spent the last twenty years raising a family with my husband. I told myself at nineteen years old that whatever it took, I would do."

"Do you think maybe by putting everyone else's needs first, you lost sight of your own? And of yourself?" Sonja was certain of it, but Belle couldn't see it. Not yet.

"I'm just living as any mother and wife would do," Belle stated. "Aren't I?"

"We're all different," Sonja told her. "But, when you look in the mirror what do you see in the reflection staring back at you?"

Belle giggled, nervously. "A woman who sometimes still feels like she's nineteen and disappointing people. Especially lately. I let my sister down because I didn't see what was right in front of me, the night she needed me more than she ever had. My kids are unhappy. Their dad moved out, because of me. My husband doesn't recognize me anymore, and I can't say that I blame him. So, this image, staring back at me is someone who's forty years old with laugh lines, crow's feet, and sun-spots. She has twenty extra pounds on her body that she's blamed on carrying three children. So, you asked, what do I see when I look in the mirror? Someone I'm not sure that I like, much less love."

"Why? Because you've made mistakes? Because you're a real woman with a busy life and calories and exercise sometimes have not been a top priority?" Sonja asked, and continued to speak. "Those are copouts. You're human. I'm not accepting those as excuses for you to not love and accept yourself for who you are. And, as far as disappointing people, you can't please anyone in your life until you please yourself. Do what you feel in your heart. Not what everyone will see as admirable or respectable."

Belle listened intently to Sonja offer her best advice, and every bit of it made sense. "How do I take that first step?"

"Begin by listening to yourself."

※※※

After dinner inside the kitchen, Sonja and Belle moved to the living room sofa with a second bottle of wine. Sonja made her way out of her chair and onto the end of the sofa. Sonja had not asked for help moving, she just explained how she had made a point of getting out of her wheelchair more. Just when Sonja was settled on the sofa and Belle sat down beside her, both with their wine glasses in hand, the front door opened. And in walked TJ.

His suit coat was off, his white long-sleeved dress shirt was cuffed at the elbows and his teal tie was loosened. He saw Belle immediately and never spoke a word. Sonja was watching her son's reaction as well.

TJ believed he would never see her again. And now he thought of Steph. It wasn't like he had to see her mother to think of her, but this brought back so much emotion for him that he couldn't move from where he had closed the door. This woman was special. She had transformed his mother. She had not waivered her support when Steph and he revealed their pregnancy. But, there was something else.

It was that night TJ had instructed Belle to pack his father's clothes and belongings and follow him to the clubhouse. She had, with no questions asked. TJ could still see the two of them in that clubhouse after he had put the suitcases and his father's body inside of the secret room and slid the door shut, sealing it, and locking it one final time. He took three steps back and then three forward again. He placed both of his palms flat on the wall that separated him and his father.

Belle had taken slow steps to reach his side. And when she was near, TJ fell to his knees on the floor. He sobbed for the father he lost. The father he loved with all of his heart. And the father he hated in the last minutes of his life. He betrayed his mother. He killed his baby. He was going to force him to do drugs, at gunpoint. *Would his father have pulled the trigger?* TJ would never know. When he dropped to his knees and began to sob, Belle was there. He recalled reaching for her in desperation and tightly wrapping his arms around her legs. She was wearing that long white skirt, and it was grubby in spots from their walk and being inside the unkept clubhouse. She held his head, rubbing the back of his neck with one hand. He remembered thinking how Belle must have thought he and his mother were crazy. He feared she wouldn't allow Steph to be with him anymore. Still, her support and the comfort she brought to him at that moment was something he would never forget.

"Teej," Sonja broke the awkward silence in the room. TJ then spoke as well.

"Hi, I'm sorry," he said, making eye contact with Belle. "You're just the last person I would expect..."

"I understand," Belle told him, and he looked down at his feet as he started to walk into the living room. He didn't sit down, he only stood in front of the chair adjacent to his mother and Belle.

"How's Steph?" he asked, not to be polite but because she was always on his mind. Not a day went by.

Belle attempted to smile. "Doing well. She does not know I'm here."

"So it's okay that you're here? The coast is clear now for you to reconnect with my mother?" TJ asked with a snarky tone.

MIRROR IMAGE

"Thomas Jude..." Sonja said to her son. He was a man now, but the way his mother could still say his name sometimes put him right back to his childhood.

Belle answered him. "It was for the best, TJ," she said, carefully, and knowing all too well that her daughter would disagree.

"Was it really?" TJ asked, taking a seat in the armchair he was standing in front of. This was his chance to ask questions. To find out how the last year had been for Steph. Countless times he had wanted to call her. "Has Steph not looked back? Because I have. I only wanted to protect her. That's why I agreed to let her go. She had been through enough."

"So have you," Belle told him, sincerely. "But, your mother has told me good things, how you are running the fashion business, and have made some significant changes..." Belle refrained from being more detailed. There was no need to bring up the drug dealings or the fact that the company was now potentially millions in debt.

"We have a long way to go," TJ admitted.

"I'm sure your efforts will pay off," Belle said, trying to encourage him, but knowing Sonja wanted him to go back to school for the education in forestry that he was interested in.

"I'm torn to see it through or not. My year has expired there, according to my mother," TJ said, appearing to soften a bit toward Belle. Seeing her again had brought back such a rush of emotions for him.

"I want you to get that college degree you were inspired to chase," Sonja told him, and Belle smiled at them both. They cared so much for each other. TJ had sacrificed so much to protect his mother, and all of them really. Four people knew what really happened to Wade Morgan that night, and they each carried some guilt and regret from it. Everyone else just assumed he ran away from trouble, and really didn't think twice. Or care.

"It will happen if it's supposed to," TJ told his mother in front of Belle. "I'm just not sure about my life's direction in any aspect right now." TJ stood up in front of the chair he had been sitting on. "I will let the two of you catch up. I'm going to get a workout in before dinner."

Sonja told him the chef had left his dinner on the stovetop, and Belle spoke one more time before TJ attempted to leave the room in a bit of a hurry. "TJ, thank you for all you've done to protect us." Belle spoke no further words. The rest was understood.

TJ looked back and nodded his head and attempted to smile. He left the room then, and yes, he was in rush. It was long overdue. He had fought it too many times. There was urgency to his actions. Maybe he was afraid he would talk himself out of it. Change his mind.

TJ was walking through the corridor of the mansion, leading to his bedroom. He had taken his cell phone out of the front pocket of his black dress pants. He kept her number. He touched the screen where he read her name. Steph Madden. Just seeing that on his phone, daily, oddly had given him some sort of comfort.

MIRROR IMAGE

I need to see you, was the text that he sent.

Chapter 22

As her plane landed at Portland International Jetport Airport, Belle was thinking about the advice Sonja had given her. Mainly, to accept and love herself first. Then, to find what makes her happy.

She had a forty-minute drive from Portland to Brunswick ahead of her and when she did arrive in the city she had always lived in, she didn't go home first. She made her way to the in-town park, located on the banks of the Androscoggin River just below the Florida Power Hydroelectric Dam. Sammy had played soccer there countless times and each and every time Belle had admired the scenic view of the river from a distance. Fishermen on the bank. Canoes and kayaks portaged around the dam. She used to think, but keep to herself, how nice it would be to just take a walk through the beautiful landscape, on that path of both greenery and color. Or, to just to sit down underneath the pergola and think. That, in particular, now reminded Belle of the backyard at the Morgan estate. When she left Sonja this time, they exchanged phone numbers and email addresses and vowed to do more than just keep in touch once in awhile.

Belle parked her SUV and walked around to the back tailgate to unzip her overnight bag and retrieve her large, floppy, beige sunhat. She had packed it, folded it compactly, and placed it neatly on top of her clothing, just in case there would be time to lounge poolside at a hotel where she originally planned to stay.

The floppy hat and its extensive brim concealed not only the top of her head, but all of her forehead and down to the base of her neck. Belle loved the protection she received from it. Not only from the sun's rays, but from the world around her. She was now thinking if she were to share that detail with Sonja, she would analyze it. *Stop relying on crutches and shields. Let your guard down.*

Belle began walking. It was midday in the middle of the week and the park was not active except for a young couple, in work attire, sharing lunch underneath the pergola. She had taken off her sweater shell she had worn on the plane. Now, she was in a sleeveless button-down powder blue blouse with a generous collar, and fitted white cropped pants. She had worn flat white strappy sandals for the walk through the airport and kept them on now as she walked throughout the park's landscape.

She savored everything on that quiet stroll. Nature relaxed her, and she had never truly realized that before. She had not taken much time for herself, to do something she enjoyed. Forty-five minutes passed before she reached the bank. It was free of activity at the moment as there were a few canoes and paddle boats that had already launched from it and were floating within eyesight on the water. Belle sat down where she was standing. She could feel the sun on her bare shoulders. The sky was clear except for three puffy white clouds.

Belle took off her sandals and set them down on the wooden bank beside her. She dipped her pale pink polished toes into the water. It felt like heaven. And then she looked up at those picture-perfect clouds again and wondered just how far beyond them was that place called heaven. *And was Gabi there?* She pulled the large brim of her sunhat lower to further conceal her eyes which now had tears welling up in them. She was doing it again, hiding her emotions, and she realized it this time. *From who? There was no one else around.* Belle was alone and apprehensive to express the sadness that overwhelmed her whenever she thought of her twin sister.

"They say when people die, they don't entirely go away, they are always with us," Belle spoke aloud and alone. "If that's true, why can't I feel you?" She sighed, and immediately shrugged off that belief. She desperately missed the connection she shared all of her life with Gabi. Believing they could still be linked was absurd.

※※※

Belle walked into her house, her skin still warm from the hot sun. She set her handbag and overnight bag on the floor beside the kitchen pantry as soon as she stepped into the door leading in from the garage. The kitchen was tidy, and the house was quiet. Steph had texted she was home from college the same day that Belle arrived in Silver Spring. She was aware that her mother had gone to see Sonja, but she had not asked any questions. She was afraid to. The feelings she still had for TJ were not leaving her heart, no matter how hard she tried. Belle had noticed no cars on the driveway or in the garage so she assumed Steph was out and maybe she had taken Skylar and Sammy with her. Belle expected Clint to arrive after work. He knew she was coming home today, but she had not given him an approximate time.

She thought about texting her children to see where they were, but before she attempted, she heard the garage door opening. She waited, and Clint walked inside the kitchen door she had just come through.

He was wearing his business attire, today it was the dark blue suit with a solid pewter tie. He looked down at her bags on the floor by his feet as he closed the door. "Did you just get in?"

Clint asked her.

"I did," she replied.

"I'm taking a late lunch. There are some leftovers in the fridge," he began to explain as he walked further into the kitchen and took off his suit coat and hung it on the back of one of the kitchen chairs.

"Go right ahead," Belle said, feeling awkward. *It was still his kitchen too.*

"So, your trip, just overnight...was it good?" Clint's words seemed awkward as well.

"It was. Sonja, as I've mentioned to you before, is like a soul sister to me." Saying the word *sister* suddenly pained her. "I just needed some advice. She's practicing again."

"And you had to fly all the way there to seek a few words of wisdom?" By now Clint was using the microwave to heat something that reeked of garlic to Belle. She tried not to let that sudden scent or his attitude unnerve her.

"Yes, I guess I did. We left things unfinished a year ago. I guess I just needed to see her again." Belle confided in him.

Clint was stirring a plate of pasta before he returned it to the microwave for a reheat. "So, seriously, is that body still in the so-called secret room of a clubhouse?"

"No," Belle replied. "The clubhouse is no longer standing. It was burned to the ground, purposely and controlled. There's nothing but flat land with grass and weeds growing in that spot now."

"Unbelievable," Clint said, shaking his head.

"I know," Belle answered, not wanting to think about it and still feeling like Clint blamed her for going along with that craziness. Or for going to Silver Spring at all when she knew who Wade Morgan really was. As far as Belle knew, Clint likely blamed her for the loss of Steph's baby too. She felt as if she just couldn't win with this man anymore.

He sat down at the table and began to eat the Amish noodles covered in a white cream sauce that appeared sticky from being overheated in the microwave. Again, the smell disgusted Belle. She never cooked with garlic. She was repulsed by the scent coming out of people's pores after eating it. Clint, she thought, knew that about her. *But, then again, had he ever really listened to her?*

"Do you want some? There's more in the container in the fridge," he asked her and then she had her answer. *No, he didn't listen.*

"I'm good. I'll have some dinner with the kids later. Where are they by the way?" she asked, standing with her back up against the counter, while he faced her as he ate from his plate in front of him on the kitchen table, occasionally pausing to drink the bottled water he had retrieved from the refrigerator.

"Sammy is at soccer camp, Skylar is at the pool with her friends, and Steph left soon after she arrived home yesterday. Something about a friend who needed her." Clint wiped his mouth with a napkin as he spoke.

"So you mean she never stayed the night at home?" Belle needed more information.

"No, as I said, came and went. I'm sure she'll check in tonight." Belle wanted to roll her eyes, but she refrained. Their daughter was twenty-one years old now, and she knew Clint would remind her of that if she persisted.

"Would you like to join us for dinner tonight?" Belle asked, hoping he would open up to giving them a chance again. He looked at her for a moment as he pushed his empty plate away from him and sat back in his chair.

"We probably shouldn't send the kids mixed signals," he stated, sounding just as unsure as he felt.

"Well we are still married," Belle said, boldly. She didn't want her comment to push him in the wrong direction. The last thing she wanted was for him to file and move ahead with divorce proceedings. "Or, maybe you would like to have dinner, just the two of us?"

This time his silence was longer. "I don't know where we go from here," he admitted.

"We could start by meeting each other halfway," she suggested. "I am more than willing to try to make this work. I never wanted you to leave."

"There will be conditions, Belle," Clint spoke adamantly, and she felt pressured to walk the line again. Follow his lead. *Was this a partnership, or familiar stomping ground where she just did as he said to keep him happy, believing she was happy, too?*

"Such as?" she dared to ask, as she folded her arms across her chest.

"The drinking. The fly by the seat of your pants attitude. We have children to raise. You can't just jet off on a whim. You never used to be that selfish." Clint's words stung.

"Selfish?" she asked him. "It's not selfish to meet one's own needs. It's healthy and if I'm going to be any good to my children, and to you, I owe it to myself to take care of me as well, and sometimes first."

"Sounds like your shrink friend may have convinced you of a few things," Clint spoke and then laughed under his breath. He was mocking her, and Sonja. *And this was the life she wanted back? The husband she wished with all of her heart would return to her?*

"She certainly did," Belle said, stepping away from the counter and beginning to leave the room.

"Hey, wait, are we finished here?" Clint was referring to their conversation about dinner plans or maybe even their future together. *If she agreed to his conditions.*

And Belle turned around, looked directly at him, and responded, "Apparently we are."

Chapter 23

Twenty-four hours ago, Steph had driven to Portland to the airport to meet TJ when his plane landed.

When she received his text, *I need to see you,* her world stopped. Steph had known her mother went to see Sonja, and her first thought was she had arranged this. Steph's response to his text was, *And I want to see you.* A few seconds later, TJ called her.

They talked for two hours on the phone about everything that happened in their lives in the last year. TJ hoped he wouldn't scare her away when he told Steph that his father's remains were gone forever. And their secret had died with him.

Steph had shuddered at the thought of that clubhouse and a dead body going up in flames. That place, and that evil man, changed her. She still grieved for the baby she had not carried for very long in her womb, but continued to carry in her heart. But, something altered for her when TJ contacted her again. She had a sense of peace for the first time ever. And she wanted to hold onto that for dear life.

The two of them embraced at the airport as soon as they caught each other's eye. They were in each other's arms at long last, standing in the middle of people coming and going in all directions. The world had not stopped for them, but it felt as if it had.

They checked into a hotel in Portland and had been in their suite since yesterday. They talked until they thought they would run out of words, but then there was more to say. Steph told him how her parents had separated and home just wasn't the same anymore. She thought of staying on campus all summer long and was still contemplating taking a full course load to also get a jump start on her medical classes. And that's when TJ had a better suggestion, or so he thought.

"Take the summer off and spend it with me," he told her, and she reminded him that he was consumed with running the fashion business. He suggested he could quit, or take a leave of absence. And that's when Steph hushed him. She made him promise not to make any rash decisions. She blamed his enthusiasm on feeling exactly as she did. They were reunited. And it seemed as if anything was possible. At least it did for a little while.

But, for Steph, she began to feel like living in that moment and revisiting who they were together was sadly comparable to going back somewhere from the past and finding it was not the same. Time had changed their relationship. Circumstances made it feel *different*.

✷✷✷

Belle had dinner with all three of her children, in their home, the following evening. It was summer break for both Skylar and Sammy, and Belle's job as a guidance counselor also allowed her the three months off. Steph returned to Brunswick a few hours earlier, and she stayed true to the story that a college friend needed her help, so she had spent the night with *her*.

The time with her children was effortless while they ate grilled cheeseburgers and mixed vegetables, and shared lighthearted conversation. Sam had concealed the vegetables under his napkin on his plate before he asked to go outside to play basketball on the driveway. Skylar said she wanted to FaceTime a friend upstairs in her bedroom, and Belle knew she liked a boy in her class and he liked her, too. As she left the kitchen, Belle reminded her to leave her bedroom door open upstairs. That was one way Belle could see and hear what was going on, if she needed to.

Steph helped her mother clear the dishes from the table. Her tan skin in faded cut-off denim shorts and a sleeveless peach v-neck cotton t-shirt clung to her full chest and flat torso.

Belle had noticed how Steph had lost weight again. In the last year, since the forced abortion, her appetite came and went.

Belle was wearing a white eyelet sundress with cap sleeves that ended at her knees. She had gone out to the river bank again today and now liked the color her skin was slowly becoming. She didn't have Steph's olive skin tone, which she had inherited from Clint, but her ivory tone was beginning to brown.

"So, tell me, were you able to help your girlfriend?" Belle asked Steph, knowing the two of them needed this time alone to talk. She was sure Steph would want to know how her visit back to the Morgan estate went.

Steph sat back down at the kitchen table. The dishes were on the counter, and Belle turned around to see why she was seated again. "I wasn't with a friend," Steph spoke, pulling her left leg up onto the chair, underneath her bottom. "TJ called me. I met him at the airport in Portland." Belle felt as if she should not be surprised. She had only seen TJ once at the mansion, and he had asked multiple questions about her daughter. "We stayed overnight in a hotel."

Belle sat down again at the table. She would not judge her daughter. It may have been an abrupt and poorly thought out plan one year ago, but ceasing all contact between them was the best she and Sonja could come up with. A murder was covered up. Talk of it amongst themselves would have put all of them at risk. Then, Belle also believed her daughter needed space and time.

"I saw him, too," Belle told her. "briefly, the night I

stayed at the mansion. Sonja is doing so well, but you probably already know that now."

"I don't want to talk about his mother," Steph stated. "I want to tell you why I agreed to meet TJ." Belle nodded her head as Steph continued. "When he contacted me, my world came to a freaking halt. I had been waiting for that man to reach out to me for what felt like forever. I knew if we could just talk, and hold each other again, I would feel complete." Steph moved her leg out from underneath her and planted both of her bare feet and peach polished toes onto the large-tiled maroon flooring divided in the cracks with black grout. She was fidgeting in her chair and finally crossed her legs and sat still again. "He asked me to marry him…"

Belle sighed. As with their relationship before, the two of them were moving entirely too fast. She made a point to look at her daughter's left hand. There was no ring on her finger. "Steph…do not make rash decisions. There's time. You just now declared your major with plans to attend medical school." As if Steph needed to be reminded. But, that's just what mothers do.

"I did make a decision," Steph replied, "and I know it's the right one for me." Belle was ready to lend her support, and top it off with her blessing. And then Steph spoke again. "My answer was no. I cannot be TJ's wife. Not now. Not ever."

"I don't understand," Belle admitted, feeling like she had missed something.

"I didn't at first either," Steph began. "I was expecting to fall back into his arms and his world so effortlessly. I do love him, and I know I always will. It just didn't feel the same with him anymore. I've changed. He's changed. And, I guess, together we're not the most magical fit anymore. I tried to explain that to him. It's like going back some place you used to love to be and fit in so well, but once you return you find so much changed and it's just not the same feeling inside."

Belle was in awe of what her daughter told her. She had lived so much of the last twenty-one years doing the same things. Going to work. Raising children. Being married to the same man. She understood what her daughter was telling her, and she attempted to imagine it. "How do you do that?" Belle asked Steph. "How do you walk away from something familiar? How do you not just…I'm sorry, for lack of a better word… settle?"

"Mom," Steph spoke, almost feeling like she could be annoyed. "This is my life. I'm making choices for me. Not too long ago, I thought my story was written. TJ and I were going to have a baby. I loved him so much. I wanted a life, and a family with him. All this time, I tried to heal. I thought I needed him back in order to do that. Turns out, I'm doing alright on my own."

"I am so proud of you," Belle said, reaching for her daughter's hand on the tabletop. "You have no idea how much…"

"It still hurts, mom. I'm not as strong as I want to be," Steph admitted. "I know I broke his heart. He was so angry, and wounded."

"He will carry on, and so will you," Belle told her daughter. "Focus on school, and when the timing is right, you will love again."

"I think he'll be the great love of my life," Steph said, solemnly. "Maybe even the one that I let slip away. Or, maybe, it just feels like that now."

"I need you to bottle that potion," Belle told her. "I'm forty years old and I have yet to learn how to make a decision without focusing on trying to please everyone else.

"Mom," Steph said, now worrying that she was steering her wrong. The last thing she wanted was for her parents' marriage to end. "You and dad belong together. Both of you are set in your ways, and it works between you two. Doesn't it?"

"I'm not so sure anymore," Belle admitted. "I am tired of being set in this way of doing things *his* way. You have to admit, your father is a control freak. It's his way or no way. Well, I'm worn out with his way…"

Steph's eyes were teary when she told her mother exactly what she was thinking. "Then you need to do what's best for you."

Chapter 24

You need to do what's best for you.

Belle found Sammy outside playing basketball. She walked directly underneath the hoop and sat down on the concrete.

"Mom, you're in the way!" Sammy complained as he dribbled from at least a three-point shot away.

"That's the idea. Come sit," she told him as she tried to sit gracefully on the concrete in a dress.

Sammy placed the basketball down and then sat on it, facing his mother. His dark hair and dark eyes caught her eye. His father's son. "Your bangs are getting long..." she told him.

"That's what this is about? You wanted to tell me I need a haircut?" The innocence of a ten year old made Belle giggle.

"That, too," she said, still smiling at her son. "And I came out here to see how you're feeling. We haven't talked much about your dad and me not living together..."

"That's because I told you I didn't want to talk about it and I said I was fine," Sammy reminded her, and Belle said, "I remember."

"Dad has a really cool apartment," Sammy offered. "It's not too far from the skateboard park." To a kid, the little things could get them through a serious change.

"Awesome," Belle said. "So you like staying with him there?"

"Yes, because I'm with him," Sammy said, and suddenly he didn't sound ten years old anymore. "He said I can stay anytime. Is that what this is about? Did dad tell you I want to live with him?"

The wind picked up out there on the driveway and suddenly Belle felt as if it would take her breath. She managed to catch enough air again to speak. "Um, no. No he didn't tell me. This is the first I've heard of it."

"Oh..." Sammy said, and he paused, and appeared as if he wanted to crawl underneath that basketball, he was seated on, and hide. "I'm sorry, mom."

"No," she said to him. "Never apologize for telling me how you feel and what you believe will make you happy." Belle was hurting inside so terribly right now. But, she was covering her emotion well.

"Okay," Sammy agreed. "Do you wanna divorce dad?" It was a simple, direct question. *Did she or not?*

Belle's first thought was to be indecisive and respond, *I wish I knew*. Instead, she said, "Yes, I do."

MIRROR IMAGE

***

Her conversation with Skylar didn't go as planned either. Belle imagined her daughter, who looked and acted so much like her, to be clingy and even adamant about keeping her parents together. She had never dealt well with change in her life.

Belle interrupted a FaceTime conversation between Skylar and the boy she wanted to call her boyfriend. But, neither one of the fifteen year olds had taken that first leap and *asked the other out*. The awkwardness of this teenage stage had Belle breathing a sigh of relief. She wasn't ready for another daughter of hers to be giving in to those intense hormones.

"Sky, do you have a minute? This can't wait," Belle said, walking into her bedroom and sitting down on the foot-end of the twin bed. Skylar was laying on the floor, on her stomach when she told the boy, whose face Belle saw briefly on the iPad screen, that she would talk again later.

Skylar crisscrossed her legs on the gray shag carpet on her bedroom floor, and she waited for her mother to speak.

"Your dad and I have been separated for almost six months now," Belle began. "I just don't see anything changing between us." Belle admitted that carefully. The last thing she wanted to do was to ever expect her children to take sides. Even though Sammy had already chosen his side. He loved her, she knew that for certain, but he was a ten-year-old impressionable boy who adored his father more.

"That's because daddy is waiting for you to change,"

Skylar spoke outright, and Belle couldn't hide the taken aback expression on her face. "He wants the old you back. We all do…"

"Sky," Belle immediately spoke up. "I am still me. Please, clarify what in the world you mean."

"When Aunt Gabi died, you changed," Skylar told her as she looked down at the loose shaggy threads of carpet and she began intertwining her fingers in the thick fabric. "You were sad, I get that, but something else was so different. It was like your body was here but the rest of you was not. Your heart wasn't into anything. I mean, you still took care of Sammy and I, and even Steph when she got pregnant, but you weren't the same. Dad says the drinking isn't helping matters either." Belle wanted to hear her out, but she suddenly felt so unnerved knowing Clint had spoken to their children about her in that manner. "Do you think you could go back to how you were when you didn't like wine, and then maybe you and dad will be able to work things out?"

"Sky, listen, please…" she began. "It's not the wine. That is not the issue. When your father doesn't agree with something, he expects everyone else to follow suit. Namely, me."

"You used to…" Skylar added.

"Yes, I used to," Belle agreed, "but was I really being true to myself when I didn't speak up or make my own decisions? I'm not talking about enjoying occasional alcohol, honey. I'm referring to just being me. Being true to myself. I hope I've taught you that." Suddenly Belle felt ashamed. She wanted to raise children who were strong and independent but she had hardly led by example at times. She quickly reminded herself of

Steph's recent actions. *She was a strong and brave young woman.* But, Skylar, at fifteen, was still very impressionable.

"You have, mom," Skylar replied. "I just liked it better when you and dad got along and you weren't so unhappy all the time."

Belle wondered if she was unhappy. She never felt unhappy, just sad and grieving. *How could she be expected to bounce around like a bubbly freaking clown when she had lost her other half?* She was grieving for Gabi. "I'm sad, Sky. I lost my twin sister. That's not something I can just get past overnight."

"No, but it has been over a year," Skylar told her.

"I'm trying..." Belle admitted, as she willed away the tears starting to well up in her eyes.

"Can I say something without making you mad, or hurting your feelings?" Skylar asked. And, Belle thought, *why the hell not? You and your brother are on a roll tonight...*

"Of course. Anything, honey. I'm a big girl. I can take it." Belle tried to smile, but she just couldn't wholeheartedly mean it.

"Why did Gabi's death have to ruin our family? When I start to miss her, I feel mad at her instead." Belle felt terrible knowing this. To see her daughter so pained by her own feelings, and by their family being severed, was heartbreaking.

"Gabi's death did ruin so much for me," Belle told her. "Losing her ruined my *everything is going to be okay* outlook. How could things ever be *okay* again? You may not fully understand this, but twins sometimes are super close. We know what the other is going to say before they say it. We feel when the other is in turmoil. I guess I'm just trying to say that I lost a part of myself when I lost my twin sister. But, I'm slowly learning to live for me, again. Without her. I also have my children to put one foot in front of the other for. I live for you guys. With that said, I know I need to learn to live for me, too. It's a healthy way to survive and be happy. Do you understand what I'm getting at here?"

"Yes, mom," Skylar answered her, "I do. I even know what you meant when you explained your connection to Aunt Gabi. We're five years apart, but Sammy and I have a special bond. I want to take care of him. I couldn't imagine not having him around all the time, you know? But, mom, there's something else I want you to know. If you and dad get divorced, and I hope you don't, but if you do, I want to take care of you, too. I mean, I want to live here with you." Belle's heart was definitely breaking. Skylar had obviously not known Sammy wanted to live with his dad. Just the thought of making her choose between her little brother and her mother was an awful thought for Belle.

"We will worry about all of that if and when the time comes," Belle assured her. "No need to concern yourself with unnecessary worry now. Okay?" Skylar was definitely her child who easily stressed over everything.

"So are you saying you and dad still might have a chance to save your marriage?" Skylar had so much hope in her eyes.

Belle had just told Sammy that she wanted to divorce his father. Now, she was being pulled so crazily into the opposite direction. One of her greatest flaws was being indecisive. She had always relied on someone else to guide her, or make decisions for her.

"Maybe," she answered, but as soon as she spoke the word, she felt regret sink into her heart.

Chapter 25

She was back on the river bank the following day. Her girls were laying out by the neighbor's swimming pool, and Sammy was at soccer practice. A few hours to herself used to be a rarity, but now that her children were older and had their own interests, this feeling was new to Belle.

Her large brim sunhat concealed much of her face again as she sat there alone at the moment. There had been a few fishermen who docked their canoes earlier, but Belle had stayed back underneath the pergola and waited. This was her spot, and a peaceful one she had found, but it wasn't for sunbathers and that's what she looked like in her spaghetti-strapped white tank top and cut off khaki shorts. She looked down at her legs, stretched out in front of her on the wooden dock, and she thought they looked fuller than usual. She smiled to herself, remembering what Gabi would say, *Oh that's just muscle. No wonder you always could run faster than me.*

MIRROR IMAGE

What would Gabi say to her now? Her marriage was falling apart. Her children were beginning to pick sides. Gabi only lived thirty-nine years, but during every one, she seized life in all its forms. She grabbed ahold and held tighter to the moments she wished would never end. She took the time to rethink her priorities. And, it was the simple things that gave her life balance, like spending time with Belle's children. She used to tell Belle, *I really don't want the man that goes along with the packaged deal of having a family, but I sure would love to have a half a dozen children to call me mom.*

Belle sat there, pondering who Gabi was and what she had taught her. They were twins and alike in many ways, but vastly different in others. If Belle were to hold tight to the moments in her own life that she wished would never end, what would those be? *Her children staying little and innocent, and always needing her. The years in her marriage before it became mundane.* Maybe it was time to rethink her priorities. *All three of her children still needed her. And had she and Clint really listened to each other lately? Was it likely that they were about to throw away twenty-one years of marriage without even trying to save it? If it was too far gone, they at least deserve to recognize that, speak of it, and find closure.* The simple things that gave her life balance were more difficult for Belle to grasp. *Other than her children and every day with them, Belle couldn't fathom what gives her balance.* She looked up at the *sky, not a cloud up there today, and she could feel the sun beating on her bare skin. Maybe doing more things just like this, for herself, would bring a better balance to her life? A glass of wine to relax and unwind at the end of the day. A mani-pedi to feel pretty. A long walk. A dinner date with Jacobi. A phone call to Sonja.* Belle needed those things, and she was just now recognizing that. Doing things for herself would rejuvenate her for her children, and her husband. Two decades had gone by while her children and her husband had come to expect her to be some sort of superwoman. And Belle expected as much from herself. She did it all, and she never complained. She never met her own needs. She was selfless. And then she lost her sister and ironically, in turn, she began to find herself. But that's when those around her thought she had changed, or had become selfish. It was unfair to Belle.

The clarity she had just been given, right now, as she sat lost in thought, felt like a tremendous weight had been lifted off of her. She contemplated getting up, walking to her vehicle, and driving to the bank. She wanted her husband to listen to her. This was important. His work could wait. Then her eyes surveyed the water and the grounds around her. She spotted a short and stocky older man in washed out bib overalls with a torn red sleeveless t-shirt underneath, and a red baseball cap with a bent and tattered bill which sat too high on his head. He carried a black tackle box in one hand and a fishing pole in the other. Three steps behind him was a woman, who looked to be his same age and build, wearing yellow CooLots and a sleeveless yellow button-down shirt. Her clean white Keds in the tall grass were following close on the heels of her husband's tan work boots.

Belle knew they were headed to the dock, so her first instinct was to leave. She didn't want to be obvious, so she waited while they stepped onto it.

"Good morning!" The older man spoke first and then looked away as he turned back around to take his wife's hand and help her up onto the dock as she had a folded lawn chair in her hands. She grinned ear-to-ear at Belle when she made it up safely with only a slight grunt.

"Morning…it's beautiful out here," Belle offered.

"It is, but you forgot your pole!" the man stated.

Belle giggled, and responded, "Oh, fishing isn't for me."

"Me neither, honey!" the woman expressed, as she sat down on the lawn chair her husband had unfolded and sat upright for her. He moved to the edge and sat down directly on the dock with his back to both his wife and Belle. "I just tag along to keep an eye on him…" Belle smiled, and then stifled a laugh when the husband turned around and rolled his eyes, unbeknownst to his wife.

The couple was quiet for a few moments, so Belle was getting ready to excuse herself and wish them a good day. "We've been married for fifty-two years," the woman suddenly offered, and Belle smiled.

"That's amazing," she responded, wondering if she should say she and her husband have made it to twenty-one years. Barely. Considering they had been separated for nearly six months. "What's your secret?" Belle asked, partly just attempting to make conversation. And then she really wondered what the secret was to a lasting marriage.

"Keep the fights clean and the sex dirty!" the husband spoke up, without taking his eyes off the water, and both Belle and the wife giggled out loud.

"That, too," the wife added coyly, and then she seemed to turn serious. "Loving each other no matter what. Fixing what's broken. No one does that anymore," she added. "I mean, this man drives me batshit crazy, but I don't want to imagine not waking up beside him every day. We've been through the mill in our lives together, and the one constant has been our love and our loyalty to that love." Belle watched the old man fishing off the bank nod his head repeatedly without looking back.

"That's beautiful," Belle said, meaning it sincerely. She wanted to know more. *What trials had they been through together? And how do you force yourselves to come out stronger? Or does it just happen, eventually?* But, she knew that knowing those details really didn't matter. What mattered was she had to try, one more time, to reach Clint. She wasn't sure if their marriage could be saved. She wasn't naïve. She knew that sometimes two people just aren't meant to be together for the rest of their lives. Sometimes there's something better, healthier, out there. She would not deprive herself of finding *what's best for her*, as Steph had said, but she was now determined to find out if that was indeed her husband.

***

Belle told all three of her children that there was money on the kitchen counter for them to order pizza for dinner. There also was enough in case they decided to get ice cream later in the evening. She was wearing a red sundress and tan wedges with red straps to match. The dress ended just above her knees and her legs were tanned from the additional rays she had caught this morning on the river bank.

"Where are you going, mom?" Skylar asked as all three of her children were within earshot. She had not told any of them about her plans. She just went upstairs to shower and get ready.

"I have a date," Belle said, turning around to face three very wide-eyed children.

"Mom!" Sammy exclaimed his disapproval first. "Does dad know?"

Skylar looked crushed and Steph looked confused. She knew her mother better than that. Or at least she thought she did. She was still married.

"Dad does know, because he's the man I'm meeting for dinner." Belle's heart was happy seeing the smiling faces and hearing a few giggles from her children.

"Does this mean…?" Skylar started to ask, and Belle interrupted her. "It means we are having dinner. We have a lot to talk about."

"In that sexy dress?" Steph stated, and Belle laughed out loud. Skylar looked a little embarrassed and Sammy rolled his eyes.

"I've had it forever. Thought it was time to wear it." Belle smirked and Steph shook her head.

"If not before, I'll see you all for breakfast in our kitchen at eight a.m. tomorrow," Belle informed her children, and then left.

✳✳✳

When she called Clint this afternoon after she returned from the river, she initially asked him if he wanted to go out for dinner. He agreed, telling her to choose the restaurant and the time. Belle then suggested his place. She would pick up a carry-out and meet him at his apartment. She reminded him that they needed to talk, *privately*, and the last thing she wanted was for people to stare and the gossip to begin again. Clint was a big wig in the City of Brunswick. *The banker. The president of The Bank of Maine who was living downtown in the brand new apartments ever since he and his wife separated. He left her. His wife was the twin of the drug addict fashion designer who overdosed last year.* Belle loathed the rumors, and she tried to ignore them. It just wasn't easy sometimes.

Belle picked up two steak dinners with baked potatoes and garden lettuce salads, and she drove directly to Clint's apartment. She knocked once on his door with her free hand as she juggled a bag of carry-outs and a bottle of wine. *There was a reason she brought that wine with her tonight.*

When Clint opened the door, he was still wearing his black dress pants and powder blue button-down shirt from work. Belle knew he had already taken off his tie. It was the first thing he did at the end of the work day, and usually he removed it inside of his car. She recalled the infinite number of times when he would call out to her in the house as he was getting dressed for work. *Have you seen my…red, yellow, blue, tie?* And she always answered the same, *Check the seats in your car.*

"Oh, hi," he said, trying not to size her up in that red dress, which he had seen hanging on their bedroom door. The price tag was still on it for months on end. He, one time, asked her *why she had not worn it or why she didn't just put it away in the closet?* Belle's response had been, *I'm saving it for something special. I'm afraid if I hang it away, I'll forget about it.* "I was about to change first, but it looks like I'll be underdressed if I do."

He stepped back and she stepped inside. He took the carry-out bag from her and glanced at the wine bottle in her hand without saying a word. Belle followed him into the kitchen. She had only been there once before. Clint had always come home to pick up, drop off, and spend time with their children. His kitchen had black-tiled flooring, and all stainless steel appliances. His countertops and kitchen table were all made of solid black granite. Even the kitchen chairs were all black. It was ritzy and expensive, and so fitting for Clint's taste.

"We should eat before our food gets cold," Clint suggested, and Belle noticed the table was already set for the two of them.

"Steak dinners from the Chop House," Belle told him as he opened one of the two carry-out containers.

"It's been awhile," he told her, as she sat down across from him at the table.

"It has," she said to him and he stood up, remembering they needed drinks. Belle had set the wine bottle down on the middle of the table, but Clint had continued to ignore it.

"What can I get you to drink?" Clint asked her.

"Water is fine," she responded, and he filled two glasses with ice and water for them.

They began eating and Clint spoke first. "How are the kids? Steph told me since she's been home that she may only spend a week or two with us and then go back to campus for summer classes?" Clint was incredibly in tune with his children. *It was one of the things Belle always adored about him.*

"They are doing well, and yes I think she will. Med school is going to be a long haul, so she may as well get a jump on it," Belle agreed.

"What are they eating for dinner tonight?" he asked.

"I left money for pizza…and ice cream," Belle giggled.

"Ahh, I miss those late-night chocolate milkshakes," he grinned.

"What else do you miss?" Belle asked him, and his face lost that grin. It was such a serious question. And she wondered if he really knew what she wanted him to say.

"Being with my family, day and night," he admitted. "My own bed…with my wife in it."

Belle attempted to smile. Her heartbeat had quickened. She watched him cut the meat on his plate, put the fork up to his mouth, and then wipe his lips with his napkin. He was conscientious of food on his face, or in his teeth. His thick dark hair was always neatly combed on his head. He rarely did not smell of cologne. He was a pretty boy, nonetheless, but Belle had come to appreciate his attention to those details. He wasn't a man who liked to hunt or fish or work on cars. He did like to be outdoors to work in the yard or grill a delicious meal. He enjoyed the sun, just as Belle did.

"Clint..." Belle started to say in response to his heartfelt openness.

"Don't. Please let me say something first..." he said, taking a drink from his glass foremost. "I know you have been grieving and will continue to grieve for the rest of your life. We all loved Gabi, but no one like you. I get that. I get all of that, Belle. I just need my wife back. My kids need..."

"Our children have me and will always have me," Belle clarified for him, and Clint nodded. "But, I think we both know why I'm here tonight. We need to talk. We have to meet in the middle here. Do we want to save our marriage or gracefully let it go?"

"That bottle you brought..." Clint pointed to the Chardonnay on the tabletop in between them. "Why? Are you flashing it in my face? Can you seriously not go a meal without drinking?"

Belle took a deep breath and paused before speaking. "I brought it with me on purpose. Not to make you angry. Not to sip it down, one glass after another, in front of you. I brought it here, tonight, to help you see that I'm not your father. A glass of wine will not turn me into a miserable, mean drunk. Your words, not mine," she reminded him. "I'm not popping the cork tonight. I don't want any. But, if I do, tomorrow or the next day, and if you're there, because I sure do hope you will be there by my side, giving our marriage all you've got right alongside of me, I want you to be okay with it. I want you to stop judging me based on your past. Stop telling me what to do and when I should do it. I know I've relied on you to make decisions, and I still will for many things. But, I'm also going to respect myself enough to make my own choices. Can you do that for me? Can you learn to take a step back and allow me to do and be what I've never allowed of myself before?"

"I'm not sure I entirely follow all you are saying," Clint admitted, "and what you're asking of me I'm not even sure I've realized any of that. We've just learned to exist year after year in our marriage, doing the things we were supposed to do, or had to do. I guess I never thought, not once, that you were doing something you didn't want to do. Were you that unhappy?"

"No, no, not at all," Belle was quick to reply. "I just need to be happier, if that makes any sense."

"A little," he said.

"Thank you," Belle said to him. She had set her fork down minutes ago. She didn't feel like eating more. She wanted more of this open conversation with her husband. "I want to be married to you. I want the next twenty-plus years to be different, but better."

"Better?" he smiled almost in disbelief at first. "We have three extraordinary kids. We have careers that have allowed us to afford to live in an amazing townhouse and we drive brand new top-of-the-line vehicles. If you want new clothes or shoes, just buy it. I mean, I know you are way thriftier than I am, but Belle the money is there." That was Clint. He could get caught up in being materialistic. And he had. For years.

"I love our life together. I appreciate how you have taken such good care of us and our family," she told him. "I just need us both to put more effort and more interest into each other." Belle knew she was guilty of that as well. She had taken him for granted. *And just like the older couple on the fishing dock near the river bank, they drove each other batshit crazy. But their love had withstood everything. They paid attention to each other. And still adored each other.* There were so many questions running through Belle's mind, but the one that she kept going over and over again was, *Was their love for each other enough?*

"I want to try, I mean, I'm willing if you are," Clint told her. He had eaten more off of his plate than Belle had, but they were both more focused on this serious conversation they were sharing. Belle nodded her head, and she felt teary. "When you asked to meet tonight, to talk, I thought for certain you wanted a divorce. I haven't gone there. I didn't want to be the one to end our marriage." This was a surprise to Belle because he was the one who left her. She continued to listen to him explain. "And then I saw you standing there, in that red dress. You don't wear red. You put that on for me tonight. That sexy, new, never-once-worn dress that hung on the back of our bedroom door longer than it was on the rack at the department store, was one you were saving for something special," he smiled at her. "I can't believe I'm your something special."

By now Belle had given in to those tears. She stood up from the table, in search of a tissue and Clint rose to his feet as well and met her as she turned into him. He placed both of his thumbs underneath her eyes and wiped away her tears. She smiled at him, still crying, and he looked into her eyes and got a little lost. It almost felt like the first time he saw her. She was beautiful. He had loved her so much. *But had he ever really told her that?* He moved closer to her, and she to him. Their lips met gently. He could taste the tears from his wife's lips. He intertwined his tongue with hers and his entire body ached for her. She, in turn, had felt a passion she wasn't sure she ever appreciated before.

He kissed her harder and deeper. On her lips. Behind her ear. Down her neck. Her arms were around him, her fingers running through his thick dark hair. She wanted to dishevel those perfectly styled hairs. She wanted to touch him everywhere and experience a passion and desire that she, as his wife, really had not truly found with him.

She made the first move to roughly pop open his shirt, and a few buttons flew off and bounced at her feet on the black-tiled flooring. She smoothed her palms over his bare chest. He moved the thin straps of her dress off of both of her shoulders. He reached behind her and unzipped her red dress. It started to fall to her hips and revealed the strapless red bra she was wearing. It had been a little snug when she put it on and so her full breasts were spilling out of the top of it.

"You do know you're making me crazy," Clint told her, standing there with his shirt entirely unbuttoned. She giggled and instantly met her lips with his. He put his hands on her breasts and then pulled down her bra. She took off his shirt and reached down for his belt buckle. By now that red dress had fallen to the floor. She was wearing a red thong, too. Belle was not the type to match her underwear, or wear anything lacy, but tonight she hoped things would get this far with her husband. She slipped out of her wedges and Clint kicked off his shoes and took off his socks. She watched his dress pants also fall to the floor as she reached for him and practically tore off his gray boxer-briefs. She touched him and he eagerly pulled off her thong. They were standing naked in that kitchen he never wanted to call his own. It was an apartment. Away from his family. Away from *his wife.*

Belle moved down to her knees and took him into her mouth. She hadn't done that before. He had asked her to, probably twice in their marriage, but she just didn't do that sort of thing. Clint began to moan. He had his hands on her head, his fingers running through her hair. She liked pleasing him. And she was. Repeatedly. He dropped to his knees and met her face with his. He kissed her hard and full on the mouth. She responded and then within seconds she had pushed him back onto the floor and straddled him. He was inside of her instantly and she rode him hard. He cried out her name just as she came too.

They were naked on an unfamiliar kitchen floor. They had never had sex anywhere but the backseat of Clint's car when they were teenagers, and then year after year only in their bed. This was definitely different, but better.

Chapter 26

At the breakfast table in the Madden's townhouse, Steph, Skylar, and Sammy all made their way downstairs and into the kitchen around eight o'clock. And each one of them was surprised and delighted to find their dad there. Both of their parents happy and in the same room as a family of five was something even Sammy knew not to take for granted ever again.

Belle had asked Clint to come home last night after they made love on the kitchen floor of the apartment he was renting. They slept in *their* bed together at the townhouse for the first time in several months. At first, Belle wondered if it was just the excitement of being together again and she supposed that was why she could not fall asleep. Her mind raced. Her heart should have been full. *Right? Wasn't that how it was supposed to feel? She will get there,* she told herself. She didn't want to disappoint her children. Or, Clint. He was more attentive to her than she ever remembered him being. And she hoped and prayed that would last. *And that their marriage would last, as well.*

Steph observed her mother in the kitchen. She was smiling, but not in her eyes. She was talking and laughing, but she appeared to be forcing her emotions. This worried Steph, and when she finally got her mother alone, she called her out on it.

"What's going on with you?" Steph asked Belle as she was ascending the stairway. They climbed the stairs together and Steph pulled her mother by the arm and into her bedroom. Steph closed the door behind her and Belle looked concerned for her now. "Talk to me, mom. Has anything really changed between you and dad?"

"Of course, honey," Belle spoke, suddenly feeling worried that her true feelings were surfacing. She just needed more time. Her marriage was going to prevail because both she and Clint were going to work at it.

Belle sat down on the foot-end of the bed while Steph kept standing. "I want to share some details with you about the time I spent with TJ in that hotel room." Belle looked confused but kept silent. "We did so much talking about all that had happened when we were apart, and all that we wanted the future to hold for us. We cried for the baby we lost. I wanted so badly to share the happiness and contentment I could see in TJ's eyes. I used to, I could again. Right? It would just take time." Belle was listening intently now. Her daughter could read her mind, and knew her heart was painfully unsettled. "The harder I tried to force it, the more unsettled I felt. Sometimes, mom, we can't go back. We cannot rekindle something lost. It's not the same. It might not even be healthy anymore. I slept with TJ that night. I hoped and I prayed that being with him would bring back my feelings. He touched me, he kissed me, we were together. And then I cried."

"Oh honey…" Belle stood up and wrapped her arms around her daughter. "I am so sorry."

"No, it's okay. I walked away when I knew I should have. It wasn't easy, it still hurts sometimes, but I am happy and just amazingly content with myself for the first time in a very long time." Steph was hoping her mother was taking her words to heart.

"Why do you not want me to be with your father?" Belle bluntly asked her.

"It's not me who doesn't want you to be with him anymore. It's you. Can you honestly tell me otherwise? What you did last night was unfair. To dad and to yourself. I mean, come on, mom! You put on this sexy dress that you never have worn in your life and you seduced your way back into your marriage!"

"That's not how it happened!" Belle raised her voice. She felt angry but she wasn't truly angry with Steph. She was upset with herself. She was frustrated because Steph was right. "I want to work things out with him. I want him to bend and I will, too. I love him."

"I know, mom. I've been there. It may not be the same, because you and dad have twenty-one years and a family at stake. But, for me, wanting to be with someone and not feeling it is all the same no matter how many years have gone by." Steph walked out of her bedroom and abruptly closed the door. She left her mother sitting there, alone. She wanted her words to sting, and they had.

MIRROR IMAGE

✳✳✳

    Two weeks went by. Steph had gone back to college for her summer school courses. Sammy was busy with various sports camps. Skylar was spending a lot of her time with her friends, and her new boyfriend. Clint was working nine and ten-hour days at the bank. And Belle had thrown herself back into being as she used to be. The mother who bent over backwards for her children, and the wife who obliged. Clint had pretty much returned to his old self. The more Belle resumed doing for their family, their house, and him, the more he in turn expected of her. The only thing that had changed between them was the sex they were now having on a regular basis. While they were limited to behind the locked door of their bedroom as they had children present in the house, their positions had changed and they often ended up on the floor beside their bed. Belle enjoyed being with him. And she did love him. Spending the rest of her life with Clint Madden wouldn't be something she absolutely could not do. And that, afterall, was Belle's prerogative.

✳✳✳

    The entire summer seemed to pass by in the blink of an eye. Belle did feel refreshed and ready to return to being a junior high guidance counselor. She was thinking of Jacobi, and how she had not returned her most recent call, as she got out of her vehicle at the park and began walking toward the dock. She had gotten used to the regulars there and it didn't feel as awkward for her if someone was fishing or canoeing near her. Today, from a distance, she saw a fisherman already on the dock. As she neared her spot, she remembered the older man in bib overalls, a ball cap, and work boots. He was alone today and Belle wondered where his sidekick was. She had been both touched and humored by them that one day. That was a day she had been at the dock, looking for answers. Now, she didn't feel as if she was seeking to make a decision about her life. She was just living it day to day, mainly for her children.

After stepping up onto the dock, Belle caught the attention of the fisherman. "Howdy," he said, and then turned back to the water as he was sitting on the edge of the dock.

"Hello," Belle said to him as she found her spot, the midway point on the dock's surface. A few minutes passed, and Belle spoke to him again. "No lady to keep an eye on you today?"

There was a long pause, and Belle wondered if he had even heard her words. Then, he pulled his fishing pole out of the water, set it right down on the dock beside him and turned around to face Belle. His knees were bent, his boots looked a little damp from dangling his feet too close to the water. "This is the first time I've been fishing since my wife and I saw you here," he began, and Belle listened. "It was a rough summer together."

Belle suddenly felt sorry for him. For the sweet couple she had only seen together once. But, she didn't want to jump to any rash conclusions.

"My wife died two days ago," he said, solemnly, looking down at his wet boots and his pant legs rolled twice above them.

"Oh...no. I am so sorry," Belle wanted to ask if she was sick. She had not appeared to be that day.

"Thank you," he replied. "We had a good run."

"I'll say, more than fifty years is remarkable!" Belle couldn't remember exactly what his wife had told her, maybe fifty-two or fifty-four.

"We were only married for a decade," the man corrected Belle.

"What?" Belle asked, confused, and she instantly wondered if the older man was *all there*.

"She had dementia, and one of the stories she loved to tell everyone was that she and I were married for fifty-two years. Not true. Ours was a second marriage for both of us. No children together. His and hers. I never asked her why she wanted to change our story. She wasn't in her right mind sometimes, you know. I chose to assume the years we did have together were so wonderful and happy for her that she wished we had been together all of our adult lives. No matter. She sometimes said what people wanted to hear and for some reason she wanted you to believe in a long, happy marriage."

"She did convince me of a few things that day," Belle said, remembering how she left the river bank afterward, on a mission to reconcile with her husband.

"That was my Gabi, one persuasive lady..."

"Excuse me?" Belle asked. "What did you say your wife's name was?"

"Gabrielle, but I liked to call her Gabi."

"I see," Belle smiled. *Yes those Gabis were something else.*

✳✳✳

Maybe that was Gabi's way of reaching her, guiding her, from beyond? Belle chose to think of it that way. And it was the first time she had felt as if Gabi had still been with her. It was a reinvigorating feeling. It really didn't matter how many years that couple had been married. Just the way they existed together, fed off of each other, and shared such mutual admiration, had lit a fire in Belle. She continued to want to keep her family together.

After dinner that evening, everyone had scattered to do their own thing. The kitchen was back in order, except for empty water bottles and soda cans left by her children on the counter today. All of it belonged in the recycle bin in the garage and she was headed there with her hands and arms full. She wasn't surprised to find the garage doors open and Clint on the driveway. He had gone outside to powerwash his car. Sammy was supposed to be helping, but she didn't see him out there. The water was off, and Clint was standing with his back to her, facing the hood of his car, with his cell phone up to his ear. He was wearing long cargo khaki shorts with a red t-shirt untucked and his feet were bare on the wet concrete. Belle assumed it was someone from the bank that he was consulting with, as she made her way over to the bin that stored recycled items. And that's when she overheard her husband.

Yes, she's finally back to normal. Well, I know, her sister's death certainly had a lot to do with her behavior. Let's just call it a mid-life crisis. Belle's heart sank. She felt as if he was mocking her. She remained standing in the far corner of the garage and she had not dropped any of the items into the bin. She didn't want to be heard. She wanted to know who Clint was talking to, and why he was being so hurtful toward her. *Well, as I said, you need to let her know who's boss. She'll eventually come around. And, if you're lucky bud, the sex will be way better after you reconcile.* Belle listened to her husband laugh into the phone and he continued to chuckle to himself after he ended the call.

She felt incredibly hurt, and angry, as she lifted the lid to the recycle bin and loudly dropped in all of the items she had been holding in her hands and in her arms. Clint immediately spun around and looked into the garage. She stood there, momentarily staring back at him.

"Oh, hi," he said to her, and he looked as if he wanted to say he didn't know she was out there.

"That was some conversation you were having about me…" she said, as she walked also in bare feet on the garage floor, toward him. Her legs looked tan in her jean short cut-offs with a boxy orange Brunswick Junior High t-shirt that they all had worn alike on a field trip day last school year.

"What do you mean?" Clint asked, attempting to hide his sudden nervousness.

"Who was on the phone, Clint?" she asked him.

"Dave, why?" he asked her.

"Did his wife leave him?" Belle wanted him to know she had heard everything he had said on his end of that phone conversation.

"They are having some trouble, yes," Clint said, knowing he was caught. And knowing what he had said was wrong. Or, at least, he had felt at fault because he had gotten caught.

"I heard what you said about me," as Belle said those words, she saw Sammy out on the street at the end of their driveway. He was riding his skateboard that Clint had bought him when he moved into his new apartment. There was a skateboard park nearby and Sammy was fascinated with the riders there and had wanted to learn how to ride a board. His balance was still not great, and riding the skateboard on the street was proving to be more difficult for him than at the park. Belle, at that moment, was wondering why Clint had allowed him on the road. He usually only practiced on the driveway, or when Belle had driven him to the skateboard park after Clint had moved back home. She was too focused on her anger for Clint right now to seek Sammy's attention and tell him to get off the road with his skateboard. "You are my husband, not my boss. You showed no respect for me. You said I had a mid-life crisis. You mocked my grief for my sister."

"No, it wasn't like that at all," Clint tried to defend himself.

"No?" Belle asked him. "Sure sounded that way to me." Again, Belle saw Sammy glide by on wheels at the end of the driveway. She looked quickly to see if the path in front of him was clear. There were no cars in either direction on that road, but she did see a little neighbor girl from down the street. She had just learned how to ride a bike without training wheels. She was coming toward Sammy, she was in his path, when a car turned onto their street, wrongly obeyed the stop sign as a yield, and sped onward. The car was driving in the same direction, nearly parallel with Sammy. The little girl was wobbly on that bicycle and unsure of which direction she should go. If she kept straight, she would crash into Sammy on the skateboard. If she took the curb, she would skin her knees as badly as the last time she fell. Sammy couldn't stop in time. He also had not mastered how to turn left. He was stronger and more capable of turning right. He didn't know there was a car coming alongside of him.

Belle's focus was no longer on her anger for Clint. She pushed past him as she saw what was happening down the street. She screamed for Sammy. She saw the skateboard go in one direction and her little boy's body falling, the front end of that speeding car crashing into him, and his body airborne before it hit hard in the rocks clear across on the other side of the road.

The fear. The pain. The adrenaline. All of it kicked in as Belle's bare feet met the road and she ran for dear life. Her son's life.

Chapter 27

Belle was sitting beside her son's broken body. She was not even sure how she had made it to this point without crying. Her strength was needed to pull him through, she guessed.

The doctor had just come into the hospital room and Belle could still hear the list of Sammy's endless injuries which he had rattled off. *A severely broken right arm. Broken right clavicle. Two fractures in his left pelvis. Bruised lungs. Bruised liver. And a concussion. No surgery was needed at this time. A long road to recovery lies ahead for him, and he will be wheelchair bound for months.*

At least he was alive, Belle thought repeatedly as she sat as close to him, at his bedside, as she could. She wanted to touch him, so she held his hand. It was cut and scraped and coated with patches of dried blood. At this moment, she was sure every part of his body hurt. He was heavily sedated to keep his brain at rest so it could attempt to heal from the concussion.

Clint stood behind her, with his back to her, facing out of the window on the far wall in that room. They had already said their share of damaging words to each other while they were forced to wait to hear any news about their son. *Why was he even on the road?* Belle had screamed at her husband. *Where the hell else was he supposed to ride?* Belle had no response to Clint's ridiculous question. They had a driveway. He often asked to be taken to the skateboard park. *You saw him out there, why the fuck didn't you put him back in the bubble you've always kept him in? Maybe if you would have let the boy skin his knee or get a bruise, his body would be tougher by now.* Clint's words were cruel and explosive and the more he spoke, and blamed her, the more Belle hated him.

Youth was on his side, the doctor had told them, and Belle clung to those words. Her son had just barely survived getting hit by a car and all she could think about was getting him well. His recovery was her sole focus.

Clint walked over to her, and began to speak. "I'm sorry. I was angry and I–" First of all, Belle could have counted on one hand the number of times her husband had ever apologized to her. And, second, she was angry too. And still was. She had blamed him for putting her son in danger. And she also blamed herself for being more focused on calling her husband out for what he had said about her during a phone call. If only she had let it go, and looked out for her son beforehand.

"I don't care how you feel," she spat at him. Belle was not a woman to talk back, or stand firmly up to anyone. Little by little, she was becoming bolder and stronger than she ever believed of herself.

"Sammy is going to be okay," he spoke again. "And so are we. We are a family." If that was Clint's way of telling his wife how things were, once again, *going to be*, Belle wanted no part of it. Her son would recover, yes. She would make sure of it. As for her marriage, Belle was finished.

✳✳✳

It took three and a half months before Sammy could walk again. His injuries had finally healed and his bones could now handle complete weight bearing. It had been a long road and incredibly difficult for him. He was angry at times because he felt helpless, and he was. Belle waited on her son, day and night. She pushed him when the therapists told her he could do more. She was responsible for his successful recovery, and after he took three steps on the wood flooring in their living room, she was the one there to reach for his hands when he felt shaky and worried about falling.

"Mom, we did it," Sammy said to her, and Belle had a smile on her face and tears in her eyes.

"You did it," Belle attempted to correct her son. "You're strong and you're a fighter. Don't ever doubt yourself, my boy."

MIRROR IMAGE

"I'm like you," he told her, and she questioned him with the expression on her face. It was as if she did not believe him.

"Really, mom. That's what I see in you." Sammy's words had touched her deeper than he could have ever known. She had never been called strong before. But, yes, what a fighter she had become. Life had thrown some serious struggles at her, and she had fought her way through all. In a paradoxical way, Belle had also felt like she had taken her first steps today. This was her new beginning, too. Her divorce was final. Shared custody of her children had been granted, and both Skylar and Sammy would primarily live with her in their townhouse on Freeport Street.

When Sammy settled on the white leather sofa in the living room, he was flipping channels on the television when Belle ascended the stairs. She walked up the windy staircase to the third floor and into her bedroom. She caught her image in the full-length mirror.

Staring back at her was a beautiful woman of character, grace, and strength. She was not without flaws, but she was now able to accept those imperfections as a part of who she was. She was a woman who loved herself, loved her children, and she appreciated with all of her being this life she had been given. And she was not about to ever again waste it feeling unhappy, unworthy, or lost.

Her new life was going to be unfamiliar and even difficult at times. Managing being alone with three children was not where she had imagined she would be at forty years old. Already it was different, but better.

Epilogue

Five years later, TJ sat behind his desk at Morgan Fashion, Inc. He was in charge, his father's company was now his. His plan to be an interim CEO for a year and then return to college to study forestry had never panned out. There was too much of a need for him to be at the helm of a corporation he had finally seen to new heights. Without the drug ward. His niche and newfound claim to fame for his family's fashion corporation was a clothing line his father had never used. He hadn't thought of it, and it had taken TJ nearly two years to realize they owned the rights to *Gabi*. Gabi Lange's clothing line was theirs.

Out of respect, TJ asked Belle Madden for her permission to create an entire advertising campaign in memory of a designer gone too soon. It was genius, and it brought in just as many millions as his father's illegal operation had on the third floor. Thirty percent of the royalties were endorsed to Belle, and she, in turn, had trust funds started for her children.

TJ was successful and content with his choice to remain in fashion as his career. He was able to continue to easily afford the estate, where his mother still lived. TJ, on the other hand, had built a moderate cottage on their land as a starter home for himself and his wife. They would shortly outgrow it though as their two-year-old daughter would soon be getting a baby brother. Sonja had invited them all to move in with her, but being on the grounds was close enough as TJ didn't want to impose on his mother's new life.

A year and half after Sonja had launched *Safe and Sound*, a client walked into her office. He had an appointment, but the middle-aged man with lengthy sandy brown hair didn't specify to the secretary what exactly he needed to be treated for. When Tyler Camden saw his therapist sitting behind her desk in a wheelchair, he instantly had hope that *she* could help him. He, at first, kept his tan sport jacket on. He was wearing medium-washed denim, cowboy boots, and a white crewneck t-shirt. It was a hot summer day and he didn't need the jacket but he was using it to cover up the arm he had lost in a farming accident. It had only been a year. He was still struggling and angry. He, first, sought healing from Sonja as a therapist, and eventually as a woman. The two of them had been married for eighteen months already. Belle had made the trip to Silver Spring just for the wedding. She would not have missed it.

Belle's children continued to make her burst at the seams with pride. Dr. Stephanie Madden had just graduated from medical school. Her hope was to eventually own a gynecology practice. She planned to use her trust fund, in honor of Gabi, to launch her own practice one day. For now, she was getting the experience she needed on board at the Brunswick Women's Center with the seasoned and well-established Dr. Tina Gingrich at the helm.

Skylar was twenty years old and in her second year of college at the University of Maine. She now wanted to be a kindergarten teacher. Sammy was a freshman in high school and still such a sensitive, sweet boy, and Belle hoped he would never lose that. She didn't want him to grow up to be too much like his father.

As far as Clint was concerned, money could buy happiness. He enjoyed flaunting his ritzy lifestyle and it appeared to have gotten worse once Belle divorced him. He frequently dated, and because most of the women were only after his bank account, he never formed a lasting relationship with any. He was a devoted father to all of his children, and that's ultimately all Belle cared about, regarding him.

Belle was now the Director of Guidance at Brunswick Junior High School. This job was more complex and demanding, and Belle was handling it with grace and style. She had a gift in how she reached young people, helped them through their teenage problems, and offered guidance as they were expected to begin planning for their future education and careers. She also oversaw a half a dozen counselors in her department. One, she hired three years ago simply because she had a gut feeling that he was a good man. His credentials were impressive from two different schools in Virginia. He had moved to Maine to be close to his children. His ex-wife moved to Maine to be near her family, giving him a choice to quit his job to be near his children, or travel a long distance to see them. With hopes of delving back onto his same career path once he moved, a man by the name of Sean Thomas walked into Belle's office.

Sean Thomas thought she was beautiful and professional. Belle thought he had boyish good looks and an infectious smile. He was five-nine, just an inch taller than Belle, and his dark brown naturally curly hair depicted an organized yet messy look all over his head. His body was thick, but fit, and when he moved his bangs from his eyes a few times during the interview, Belle felt smitten. She ignored those feelings, but didn't completely bury them when she hired him the following day. She could hardly wait to call him up and tell him he had a job as a guidance counselor again.

Working a few late evenings a week in the guidance office was not unusual for Belle, especially when her children were busy with sports or after-school activities. Sean had also spent a few nights at the office because he didn't have anyone to go home to. He admitted that to Belle, and she sympathized with him. And connected with him on that level for sure. Her children didn't always need her either. She felt lonely and isolated at times when Clint had both Skylar and Sammy at his apartment for a weekend, or longer. Belle made an attempt to find hobbies, and make time for her and Jacobi. Before Sonja remarried, Belle had taken several overnight trips to visit her. She adored Sonja's new husband as well. He was a country boy, and in many ways so completely opposite of Sonja. But they had found common ground in their handicaps and their relationship certainly appeared perfect. That was what Belle was looking for. Common ground. A man to have fun with, to laugh and cry with. Life certainly wasn't easy, but sharing it with someone special made it all the more worthwhile.

Laughing definitely was something Belle could do with Sean. She giggled at how he always took too many pictures of his boys on his phone. Whenever they had been together, Belle could count on Sean showing her photographs of seven-year-old Zander and five-year-old Cash. Belle had crushed on Sean, a man who worked under her, for several months. She never acted on her feelings or remotely gave him any indication she was into him. He was eight years younger than her, and Belle only chalked up her emotions to being ready to find love, but didn't allow herself to believe she had actually found him.

They worked together for two years. Shared lunches together. Whined to each other often when they dealt with their former spouse frustrations. Both of them had come to rely on the other being there.

Still, Belle assumed Sean saw her as a big sister. Or just a good friend. She was certain he indulged in romantic trysts when he was not spending quality time with his boys. A man like him shouldn't be alone. *Way too sexy to sleep alone.* Belle often had to force that thought out of her mind. As much as it annoyed her to go there in her mind, because she knew nothing could ever come of it, Belle couldn't stop. She liked how Sean Thomas made her feel. Even if it was only in her fantasies.

There wasn't much she hadn't told him. He knew about her marriage, and how long it took her to realize she was never truly happy with Clint. She always wanted to be, and perceiving she was for decades had eventually caught up with her. Sean was aware that Belle had an identical twin sister for thirty-nine years, and how Gabi's life ended. Belle spoke of her children to him often, so much that Sean felt as if he knew them.

Twenty-six months into their working relationship and close friendship, Sean spotted Belle for the first time outside of their school element. She was on the dock near the river bank. At first glance, he thought for certain that was her. Her long arms. Her broad shoulders. Beautiful long blonde hair. He never went there with her. He couldn't. She was his boss. He sure did enjoy thinking it was possible though.

Sean had been running on the trail at the park. He did frequently, and wondered why he had never spotted her there before. Maybe she didn't come there as often as he had? Maybe they were just missing each other every time? Like two ships passing in the night. Sean didn't allow himself to overthink this time. He just made his way over to the dock.

He stepped up on the dock and for a moment beneath her large brim sunhat all Belle could see was a pair of red running shoes with gray laces. She peeked from under her hat. Long red shorts. A charcoal gray tank top. Tight, thick chest and shoulder muscles. And that curly hair.

"I thought that was you..." Sean had said as he plopped down beside her, noticing her tan legs and how gracefully Belle sat there in a white, eyelet sundress that he thought made her look stunning.

"I hide under my hat sometimes," she teased, noticing he had perspiration on his hairline and few of his curls looked damp. *Sexy*. And damn how it was suddenly *hot* under the sun on that dock.

It had been ten months since that day, and Belle still recalled it fondly. That dock, alongside the river bank was where Sean Thomas had kissed her for the first time. She had never been kissed like that before. Tenderness combined with explosive passion. A passion that began smoldering from the moment they first laid eyes on each other.

✳ ✳ ✳

MIRROR IMAGE

Belle spent the following forty years as Mrs. Isabelle Thomas. Sean was her happily ever after. At eighty-five years old, every wrinkle she wore told her story.

Pregnant and terrified for her future at nineteen.

Married and submissive to a man she wanted to believe had captured her heart.

Three beautiful, perfect in her maternal eyes, children who filled her heart to the point of ache at times.

Her twin sister. Gabi was everything Belle had wished to be. Losing her broke Belle's very soul.

The rage and the hatred she carried for Wade Morgan.

The shock of history repeating itself when her daughter became pregnant in college. The forced abortion, at a Wade's hands, of what would have been her first grandbaby. Wanting to take that man's life. Aiding in the cover-up of his murder. Knowing they had gotten away with it.

Watching a speeding car strike her little boy. Begging for his life to be spared. Witnessing complete healing of his broken body.

The destruction of her marriage. Finally making the choice to end her commitment to a man who was not worthy of her.

Learning to love herself.

Accepting the mirror's image as flawed but beautiful.

Finding true and lasting love. Exchanging marriage vows on the dock, overlooking the river bank.

Belle was eighty-five years old when she died in the arms of the man she adored. She had asked Sean Thomas to take her to the river bank one last time. Her heart was weak. Congestive heart failure, her physician had said. She had lived a long, full, amazingly blessed life. Belle took her last breath, content and fulfilled. And completely at peace with a life well-lived.

ABOUT THE AUTHOR

I have a history of explaining why I've written each story at the end of every book. I reveal the one person or thing that inspired me. This story in Mirror Image was launched, in my imagination, when I thought about the makeup of people all around us, every day. We all know that person who is beautiful inside and out, but do they know it? Not usually.

Belle Madden is a character I created who very much represents the everyday woman. She takes care of her family. She excels in her career. She does what she has to do when she has to do it. She puts everyone ahead of herself. And somehow along the way she lost herself.

Belle's story unfolds when tragedy strikes her. Her makeup changes. She loses interest in the things she once cared about. But in the midst of it all, she finds herself. And she prevails stronger than before. She discovers she must make changes in order to live a fulfilling life.

As a reader, when you close this book, if you take anything with you from this story, take that. Grab ahold of the courage to face change, if you need to.

As always, thank you for reading!

love,

Lori Bell

Made in the USA
Charleston, SC
26 May 2016